MISHAPS AND MAJORS

ALEXA SANTI

Major Lord Philip Avondale had been in many a scrape thanks to his twin brother Peter, but being kidnapped in his sibling's stead was perhaps a step too far, even for a man as tolerant as himself.

A call of, "Oi! Parson!" from the street had distracted him away from a blow directed to his head, disorienting him and giving the villains an opportunity to hustle him into a waiting carriage that smelled distinctly of boiled cabbage and horse manure. Head spinning, he had been pinned to the floor of the carriage by two equally foul-smelling ruffians for what seemed like hours until they finally arrived at a house, dragged him up the stairs, and dropped him to the floor with a final kick to the ribs.

And here he was. Philip looked around the small and shabby room where they had dumped him, moving his head carefully so as not to restart its pounding again. The surrounding silence told him the house was in the country, not London. Light coming through the one small window was starting to fade. A low pallet stuffed with straw sprawled in one corner and a chamber pot sat conspicuously in the other. Hopefully, it would prove cleaner than the rest of the room.

It was still better quarters than sleeping rough on the Peninsula.

The scrape of a boot outside the door alerted him to someone's arrival, and he stood to face whoever was there. He stood too quickly, though, and had to brace himself against the nausea that followed.

The door opened, and two men entered. Complete strangers. The taller one had a shock of wiry dark hair above his gaunt features. Bright red blotches on his otherwise pale nose and cheeks marked him as a heavy drinker. The shorter one was washed-out all over: lank blond hair, dun-colored skin, watery blue eyes.

The taller one sneered at him, while the other seemed to cringe back. "Well, parson. I suppose you never expected to find yourself here."

"No, I didn't," Philip said, with perfect truth.

"It won't be for long," the other man piped up. "Just a few days."

"Do you suppose I could get a chair? Perhaps a table?" Philip gestured to the pallet. "I'll be dreadfully uncomfortable if that's the only place for me to sit."

The first man sneered again. Did he even have another expression? "This ain't a dook's palace, you know. You takes what we gives you and be grateful for it."

"Now, Dickie," the other man said, "'e's a parson, after all. A man of God ought to get some kind o' consideration, don't you think?"

Dickie contemplated this idea for a moment and then

spat onto the floor, barely missing the toe of Philip's boot. "I known more parsons than you, Jas. Ain't none of them worth a farthing."

As the two men continued to bicker, Philip saw the door open a tiny bit wider so the hunched figure of a woman could creep in. She carried a bucket and a small hand broom —a maid of all work to clean and lay the fireplace, it seemed.

Her face was turned away from him, but something about her was familiar. The way she moved, even while trying not to draw attention to herself. Her graceful figure as she crouched to clean the fireplace, the warm brown skin of her arms streaked with soot from the work. Her nimble hands, as they briskly swept the hearth.

She was doing her best not to draw attention to herself, but he *knew* her.

She glanced up at him from beneath the brim of a floppy mobcap that barely contained her dark curls. Those same thickly-lashed dark eyes still taunted him from time to time in his dreams, and his breath caught for a moment.

He had not seen her in four years, but he had never forgotten the unmistakable Junia Reynolds.

Major Avondale's presence ruined everything.

Junia Reynolds racked her brain as she briskly swept the coal dust from the grate. She had expected Dickie and Jasper to stay overnight in London as they usually did, giving her an opportunity to free her father from the room where they were holding him prisoner. A spoonful of valerian in the guards' dinner to make them doze, and she and Pappa would have had an hours-long head start.

Glancing up from beneath her mobcap, she shot Major Avondale a glare that was only strengthened by the little leap her heart had made when she recognized him. Even with his chestnut curls disheveled and dried blood tracing along his high cheekbone, he had the same air of unruffled calm she remembered from the British warship that had transported her family from slavery in Maryland to freedom in England four years ago. She had told herself what she felt for him was only a schoolgirl crush, but now she realized she had been looking for him around every corner she turned in London. It made her even angrier. Where had he been when she needed him, and why must he turn up now to complicate what she had nearly solved?

Junia ducked her head and concentrated on sweeping the hearth as she tried to discreetly eavesdrop on Dickie and Jasper, even as her body prickled with awareness of Avondale's presence. The thick London accents were still difficult for her to decipher, but they seemed to disagree about exactly what comforts their prisoner was and was not to be allowed. It was no surprise Dickie argued for harsher treatment and Jasper for a little softness. She had already seen how they treated her father.

Pappa.

Gripping the brush tighter, she pushed away the thought. She could not come up with a new escape plan if she did not stay calm and keep a clear head.

"Gentlemen, gentlemen," Major Avondale said, and she frowned a little into the flagstones of the hearth as she scrubbed. His voice was different than she remembered. He had been a commanding and self-assured officer on board the ship, not this diffident-seeming man in fashionable civilian clothing.

"Gentlemen, there is no need to argue," he continued when Dickie and Jasper subsided. "If there is no chair or table to be had, then that shall be the lot our Lord has given me."

Dickie grunted and Jasper smiled tentatively, exposing the several rotting stumps of his teeth. "I thankee, parson. But mebbe the girl can look in the attic for summat for you to sit on."

Junia hunched down under the unexpected attention, brushing the hearth vigorously one last time before she laid fresh coals in the grate.

"I would appreciate it," Major Avondale said. She could feel him glance at her, and then away.

With a murmur, she rose back to her half-crouch and scuttled away again, pausing in the hallway just out of sight to see if the conversation continued. To her disappointment, all she heard was the sound of Dickie and Jasper's footsteps towards the door, which sent her hurtling down the narrow steps back to the kitchen.

It wasn't as though there wasn't enough for her to do, even beside her plans to rescue her father. There was a guard at each of the two doors of the house, but she was the only inside servant. She was kept busy all day with the cooking and cleaning necessary for the five—now six—men in the house.

With a sigh, she pushed through the door to the kitchen, where she had left a hearty stew for the evening meal bubbling over the fire. Her skills were meager since she had been trained as a lady's maid, not a cook, but the men didn't have high standards. Plain food and plenty of it seemed to satisfy them and left her enough time to continue to assess the house under the guise of cleaning it, a job which would take a dozen maids a full week to accomplish, at the least.

Her biggest problem was the nighttime guards. Even if she and her father could both get through the small window of his room, that window was directly above the door where Robby stood all night, with the other guard, Jem, at the back. Things were a bit looser during the day while the guards slept, but then Dickie and Jasper were constantly underfoot, quarreling and sniping at each other while they walked through the house in their muddy boots and left dishes under the furniture for her to pick up. This was why she had set her plan for when they would be gone overnight… but they had returned unexpectedly, and with Major Avondale in tow.

Once in the kitchen, she set down the coal scuttle, rinsed her hands and arms under the pump in the sink, and floured the table so she could punch down the dough for the week's bread. She had to admit, the kneading and punching relieved her feelings at least a little and helped her keep a clearer head as she devised a way to get around the guards.

The man upstairs must be Major Avondale. He *must* be. She had seen the recognition on his face, as she knew he had seen it on hers. Why Dickie and Jasper thought he was a clergyman was beyond her, but she hoped she would be able to use their confusion to her advantage.

She punched the dough a little harder than she needed to. It did not matter that she knew him, or that he had been kind when she was a frightened girl on her way to a new country. She could not allow him to stand in the way of her goal.

As she had done every night since the day she had arrived in this house, Junia spooned the evening's dinner into a bowl for Robby, the younger of the two guards, to take upstairs to her father. She tried to be discreet about giving Pappa the best pieces of meat, a secret signal to him that she was still there and still working to free him. Her father was clearly the more valuable of the two prisoners since she was rarely allowed inside his room and, even then, it was under the watchful eye of Dickie or Jasper. So far, they were less watchful with Major Avondale, and she hoped to be able to turn that to her advantage.

When Robby returned with the empty bowl, Junia said, "What about the other, um, guest?"

"T'other?"

"There's a man in the other room. A minister."

Robby frowned. "Dickie didn't tell me about no other pris'ner."

"I saw him today when I cleaned the hearth," she said. "You'd better take him up a bowl, too."

"Yes, Miss Josephine," Robby said meekly, and she dished more stew out. He towered over her and didn't seem very bright, but he would sometimes follow her around like a puppy unless she sent him off to do an errand for her.

"Take it to… the minister for his dinner, and then you may have your own."

Obediently, Robby trotted off and Junia huffed a sigh to brace herself before she went down the hallway to the dining room. It wasn't much—just a table and four chairs—but Dickie insisted he and Jasper should eat there rather than in the kitchen, where she would be much more able to eavesdrop on them.

As usual, Dickie was drinking deep of the cheap gin he brought with him by the case from London, and Jasper wasn't in much better condition. As she cleared their plates, their only discussion was a drunken argument about the latest prizefight they had seen in London. She ignored Dickie's hard pinch on her bottom. He was already too drunk to do anything, and even if he had wanted more, she wedged her bedroom door shut every night to make it not worth his trouble to molest her.

"But why a parson?" Jasper whined, and Junia slowed her movements to listen as she cleaned up.

Dickie took another swig of his tankard of gin and belched. "That's the way it goes sometimes in this business. People stick their noses in where they don't belong and have to get cut out. Best not to worry about it."

"Havin' a parson around makes me feel guilty," Jasper muttered. "Like I shoulda gone to chapel like me mum wanted."

"Don't be stupid," Dickie said, and the conversation turned again until Junia felt she could not dawdle in the room any longer without drawing attention.

Back in the kitchen, she dished out stew for Robby and Jem, the other guard, and cleaned the kitchen up around them as they ate, banking the fire and preparing the ingredients she would need to make porridge in the morning.

Robby pushed his bowl away. "That was right good, Miss Josephine."

"Thank you," Junia said, a thread of nervousness creeping up her spine. Jasper and Jem were indifferent to her,

but she was starting to suspect Robby was developing…
feelings for her.

If she encouraged those feelings, it might help her carry
out her plan, make him more careless about his guard duties.
But, no, she could not bring herself to lead a man on like
that, even in the service of freeing her father. Not to mention
that it was potentially dangerous, since he was a criminal
participating in a kidnapping. Two kidnappings, now.

Junia turned away to finish her cleaning, ignoring him.
Robby hovered for a long moment before Jem punched him
lightly on the shoulder and Robby obediently followed the
other man out the kitchen door to their posts for the night.

Suppressing a yawn, she lit a candle from the banked fire
and made her way to the tiny scullery maid's room behind
the kitchen's fireplace. There was barely enough space for her
straw pallet and the chest which held an extra work dress and
a few chemises, but she preferred the windowless quarters to
a more spacious room that would be easier for one of the
men to sneak into.

She pushed the wooden wedge under the door, undressed
and washed, combed and wrapped her hair, and lay herself
down for the night, head still spinning.

As she lay on the thin pallet, memories she had pushed
aside flooded back. His profile against the setting sun as they
stood at the rail watching dolphins swim beside the ship.
Walking around and around the deck with her mother on his
arm, mesmerized by the broad shoulders inside his scarlet
uniform coat as she and her younger sister Zillah followed
behind. The way he would throw his head back and laugh
and she would stare at his strong throat, even knowing he
thought of her as a younger sister, at best. She had been

desperately infatuated, and he could not have been kinder or more remote.

After the Battle of Waterloo, she had read the published lists of the names of the dead officers over and over again, heart in her throat, relieved beyond words his name had never appeared. She knew he was still alive, and that knowledge allowed her to continue to dream that, one day, she might look up and there he would be, rounding a corner of the street to greet her, like magic. Or destiny.

She flopped onto her other side, angry with herself. She was not that young refugee any longer. The success of her father's counting-house and the support of other black Londoners had provided a comfortable middle-class life far beyond what she ever could have dreamed when her family had been held in bondage in Maryland.

So why must she now dream of even more merely because Major Avondale had at last re-appeared in her life, handsomer than ever but seemingly in a disguise of his own?

Why had they kidnapped Major Avondale? And why did they think he was a clergyman?

As Philip listened carefully that evening, he could hear movement on the other side of the wall. The one to the north, as far as he could tell.

A short murmur of voices quickly faded away. To his surprise, footsteps returned a few minutes later and the door unlocked and opened to reveal a large but dull-looking man holding a tray with a bowl and a piece of bread on it.

"She said you was to have it. Miss Josephine."

"Ah. Thank you, then." Philip took the tray and set it on the floor. The other man left as abruptly as he had arrived, locking the door behind him.

At least someone had remembered to feed him. He suspected it was all Junia. He likely could have starved for all Dickie and… what was the other name? Jas? They did not strike him as the most diligent of wardens.

He could not help but wonder again what had brought her to this pass. He had made it a point to be present when her family debarked the ship upon their arrival, giving first her mother and then her younger sister a steadying hand as they picked their way down the rope ladder to the boat that would bring them to the shores of England.

Junia had allowed her hand to rest in his for a long moment as she looked up at him, her dark eyes shimmering with unshed tears. "You've been so kind, Major. I will never forget you."

He had laughed, to conceal his own emotion. "Of course you shall, Miss Reynolds. You have a whole new life ahead of you."

Ducking her head, she squeezed his hand one last time before letting go to follow her mother and sister down to the boat. Swallowing hard, he turned and shook her father's hand with a smile.

"Goodbye, Mr. Reynolds."

"Goodbye, Major. Why not stop in and see us sometime once we get settled?"

Philip shook his head, but smiled. "I'm afraid my duties will not allow it. But I wish you and your family all the best."

Caius Reynolds had cast a shrewd glance at him before following his family down to the boat. Philip turned his back and walked away, knowing he could not bear to watch her be rowed away from him.

He would always wonder about her once she was gone from his life, but both honor and duty required him to let her go without allowing her to suspect his emotions. She was only seventeen; she would soon forget him.

The pacing began again on the other side of the wall, drawing Philip back from his memories. Up and down. Back and forth. Repetitive, purposeful, as if to fill the time. It was the deliberation of the movement that convinced him the person on the other side of the wall must be a fellow prisoner. Why else would someone pace like that, in repetitive steps which rarely seemed to vary?

If there *was* another prisoner, a possible reason for Junia's presence in the house occurred to him in a flash.

Philip waited until the coals in the fire burned low and all sound in the house died down to tap experimentally on the wall, rapping twice in quick succession, pausing, and then repeating the two raps, trying to make it loud enough for the sound to reach through the plaster but quiet enough not to be heard by the guards below the window.

There was a long pause. Then a series of soft footfalls to the wall.

Two raps in response, then a pause, then two more, in the same quick succession.

If one of the kidnappers had been the man in the other room, they would have shouted at him to quiet down, or even burst into the room to silence him. Only a fellow prisoner would be interested in communicating.

And Philip now had a suspicion as to who it could be.

$\approx$ 2 $\approx$

As she usually did, Junia rose before dawn and made her way down the short passageway to the kitchen, shivering in the early morning chill. Yawning, she poked at the kitchen fire to bring it back to life, feeding in more wood until she was rewarded with a steady flame. It had been a difficult night's sleep, her fear for her father and for her family back in London now joined with fear for Major Avondale.

The homely tasks soothed her as she moved around the kitchen, bringing the porridge to a simmer and putting the teakettle over the fire. Those who disliked porridge could slice themselves some bread and cheese from the pantry, assuming the mice had not gotten to it. She wished she had one of her mother's thick knitted shawls to keep her warm, but it was exactly the sort of possession the impoverished maidservant she claimed to be would never have.

She prepared a tray for her father, adding a cup of strong tea in a chipped earthenware mug, and carried it upstairs to where Jem stood outside her father's door. With a nod to her, he unlocked it and stood back so she could carry the tray inside.

Caius Reynolds was already sitting at the desk, an open account book in front of him, carefully tracing his finger down the row of numbers and consulting the list next to him. She knew nothing of his task but that Dickie and Jasper brought him stacks of accounting books to alter using written instructions. Each set of completed books were taken away and replaced with more in an endless-seeming supply.

She worried what would happen to him when the supply ran out.

She set the tray down on the desk and he looked up to smile at her. Junia flashed him a tiny return smile before turning away, her heart aching. It had only been two weeks, but he already looked a little ashen, drawn and faded by the imprisonment and lack of exercise. She knew he paced the room to pass the time, but it could never replace the long walks through the streets of London her father preferred.

To her surprise, he touched the back of her hand, too swiftly for Jem to see, and she looked back at him. Her father gestured to the far wall with a raise of his eyebrows and then held her gaze. It took her a moment to understand what he was asking before it dawned on her, and she nodded once in confirmation.

Yes, there is another prisoner in that room.

Her father nodded and returned to his account book. Junia held back for a moment, checking again that he seemed well, before reluctantly leaving the room, Jem locking the door behind her.

She *would* get him out, no matter what it required.

PHILIP LOOKED up as the door unlocked and opened, trying to keep his expression mild. One of the villains—the one called Jas—stood in the doorway, cap snatched off his greasy hair and twisting in his hands.

"Morning, parson."

"Good morning," Philip said, and smiled. The man seemed to find it reassuring, because he took another step into the room.

"I was thinking… we snatched yer without yer Bible, didn't we?"

"Yes," Philip lied. "I must have dropped it when you pushed me into the carriage."

"It ain't right. A parson without his Bible, I mean. So I brung you one."

The book Jas shoved at him was filthy, the cheap cover torn and folded, but Philip tried to accept it with a believable amount of reverence. "Thank you, my son."

"'Tis nothin', parson."

Philip paged through it, trying to think as he scanned past the familiar verses. At Winchester, he had once won a prize for scripture knowledge, though the headmaster had never known Philip had hidden the answers on the inside of his cuff. The guilt over his cheating had been worth being able to lord it over Peter that Philip knew the Bible better than he did, even though Peter was the one destined for the Church and Philip for the army.

"Is there… do ye need anywhat else?"

Philip looked up, and fixed the man with his sternest vicar's gaze. "I need my freedom."

The man flinched but sighed. "Can't do that, parson. I wish I could. I really do. But I can't."

"I understand," Philip said, and then an idea dawned. "Perhaps you could send someone to build up the fire. It's a bit chilly in here."

"Ar. I can send the girl, mebbe."

"Thank you," Philip said, keeping the triumph from his voice.

He remained seated, pretending to read the Bible, as Jas exited the room, locking the door behind him. It seemed a long wait until the door unlocked again and she crept into the room, the door half-closing as Jas stepped into the corridor. Philip pretended not to watch as Junia crossed to the grate and began to sweep out the coal dust, casting glances at him as he ignored her. The fact that a run-down house like this would have coal grates rather than wood fireplaces was intriguing. They were not so far from London as he had feared if the fires in this house were made with coal rather than wood.

She kept her back to him, but he knew it was Junia. He could never mistake her for anyone else. The hem of her threadbare gown was filthy and her arms were streaked with flour and coal dust. He felt a moment of anger that she would end up a maidservant in this hovel after her daring escape from slavery, though at least the villains here were likely paying her a few pence per week.

Though it seemed more and more likely to him that her reason for being here was not because her family had fallen on hard times.

"Is he still outside the door?" he said as softly as he could. She froze, and then nodded without looking at him.

He continued to page through the Bible with one hand, the turning of the paper sounding unusually loud in the silence of the room broken only by Junia's vigorous sweeping at the hearth. With his other hand, he searched through his pockets as quietly as he could manage. They had taken his purse, of course, and his penknife, and his watch and fob were probably fetching a pretty penny with a crooked jeweler at this very moment.

But he found something more precious that the ruffians had overlooked, something far more useful than money in his present predicament—a tiny stub of a pencil with a bit of lead still exposed.

He flipped through the pages of the pocket Bible, trying to decide what to do. Writing on the pages might be too dangerous if the villains decided to search her once she left the room. He needed a code of some kind to pass a message that would not endanger her. After a long moment, he chose a psalm and began to mark it.

She finished sweeping out the grate and piling the new fuel on the fire. She looked over her shoulder at him, and he gestured for her to come closer. She stepped carefully, but one of the boards groaned beneath her feet, and the door began to swing open.

In a flash, she dropped to her knees before Philip, and he placed his hand on her head, slightly dislodging her cap as the door opened and the other villain—not the one who had given him the Bible—scowled at them both. Dickie, that was the man's name.

"Amen," Philip said, and pressed the tiny square of paper into the palm of her hand as she rose to her feet, head still bowed. He lightly squeezed her closed hand, hoping to lend her some comfort and reassurance amidst their current danger, and her fingers brushed his as he let go.

"Amen," she said, so softly he could barely hear her, and scuttled from the room under the furious eye of his captor.

"Givin' out blessings, are we, parson?" the man drawled as he sauntered into the room. Philip kept a wary eye on him. Dickie was more volatile than his partner, and Philip did not want to have to defend himself when Junia and the other prisoner were at risk. Especially if he was right, and the other prisoner was her father.

"Do you feel in need of one?" Philip said genially. "I am always willing to accept sinners back into the fold."

"None o' that churchin' for me." Dickie spat on the floor, once again dangerously close to the toe of Philip's boot. Philip kept his expression placid, though he marked the action down for future retribution. "God never did me no good."

"The door to St. Luke's is open to anyone who wants to be forgiven."

"Is that what you was doing with the girl? Forgivin' her sins?"

"She asked for a blessing and I gave it."

The man gave him a moody glare. "Wenches is all the same. Sweet on the outside, whores at the core."

Rage and fear choked Philip's throat for a long moment. After his years at war, he had an acute understanding of how much danger Junia was in for as long as she remained in this house. "She asked me to pray for her ailing mother, and we did."

"That better be all it was, 'cause maids are a penny to the

dozen. I could slit her throat, throw her in a ditch, and have another tweeny here afore the sun set."

"Understood," Philip said. Had the girl been a stranger to him, he might have taken the warning and left well enough alone so as not to endanger her further, but he had no choice. Either Junia helped him escape or they might all be murdered.

BACK IN THE KITCHEN, Junia carefully unfolded the tiny piece of paper Major Avondale had pressed into her hand. It was a page torn from Psalms—Psalm 107—and she stared at it for a long moment before she realized he'd scored small pencil marks under some of the letters.

A coded message.

The door opened behind her and she shoved the paper into the pocket of her apron to look at when she had more privacy. She turned to see Dickie standing in the doorway glaring at her.

"You'd best not be playing a game," he said, his quiet tone more menacing than any bluster she had heard from him. Knowing she was trembling, she kept her gaze locked with his, trying to keep her expression as innocent and confused as she could.

"I don't know what you mean."

"That man is here a'purpose, and you ain't. It's easy to make a woman disappear." Dickie drew one dirty finger across his throat, and her hand went to her own throat involuntarily.

"I... I won't do anything."

"You know what's in store for you if you do," he said, then spun on his heel and strode away.

Junia sank down onto a kitchen bench. She had been able to create a discreet plan to free her father, had had it just within her grasp, and within less than a day of Major Avondale arriving in the house, it was all in ruins.

He was an army officer. He could take care of himself. There was no need to put her father's life in peril just because Major Avondale was endangered as well.

Even if the thought of abandoning Avondale to his fate made her want to weep.

She smoothed her hand over her apron, and was reminded of the small book he'd given her aboard ship and how perfectly it had fit into her apron pocket.

"I can't accept it," she had protested, but he had only smiled.

"I can get another copy."

"But you said you won it at school."

A peculiar smile twitched at the corner of his mouth. "Don't worry. I cheated to win it."

She laughed, but he seemed to be serious. She turned the well-worn book in her hand to look at the spine. *The Pilgrim's Progress*.

"I would like you to have it, since you enjoy reading. Troop ships do not carry many books on board."

She hesitated for another moment, worried what her mother would say, but wanting to accept it. She took a deep breath and said with a curtsy, "Thank you, Major Avondale."

He half-bowed to her in return, gravely courteous. "You are welcome, Miss Reynolds."

She had only realized later that he must have brought the

book to war with him, carried it with him for years, and then had given it to her in a way careless enough to convince her to accept it. But she had only realized it long after they had parted.

Junia rubbed her finger against the edge of the note, pushed it deeper into her apron pocket, and began her preparations for the evening meal. Robby had wrung the neck of a chicken and bashfully presented it to her that morning, so she began the loathsome process of plucking it to prepare for roasting. She spent the rest of the day busying herself with domestic tasks, trying not to wonder what was happening to either of the prisoners upstairs.

Dickie kept a watchful eye on her throughout the day, and she did nothing to make him suspicious.

In her room that night, Junia pulled Avondale's sheet of paper close to the candle, trying to see the tiny pencil marks under some of the letters. She spelled and re-spelled the letters in her head multiple times, trying to make sense of them, sometimes mistaking a speck of dirt for a pencil mark or dismissing one as a mere speck of dirt.

But at last, she formed a sentence that made sense to her, and a wave of relief washed over her.

They meant to take my brother.

Dickie and Jasper had abducted the wrong man.

The knowledge only made Major Avondale's position more dangerous. Even as a duke's brother, it would be easy enough for the men to kill him and dump his body on Hampstead Heath, where highwaymen still roamed, and make it look as though he had been robbed and murdered. No one would be able to connect them to the crime.

No one but her.

❧ 3 ❦

The tension in the house slowly receded over the next several days. Junia was careful to stay out of Dickie's path except when absolutely necessary, and to keep her head down and her eyes to herself when she did encounter him. He seemed to feel he had sufficiently cowed her, because he returned to his carelessly arrogant way of ignoring her as much as possible.

He was still suspicious enough to ensure Jem or Robby or Jasper hovered in the open doorway whenever she delivered food to the two prisoners or cleaned their rooms. There were no further opportunities for her to have a quiet conversation with either her father or Major Avondale under those bored gazes. Not even a chance for another note to be slipped.

Patience was one of Junia's virtues, and it paid off the morning Dickie and Jasper came thundering down the stairs carrying a trunkload of ledgers gathered from her father's room. They supervised Jem and Robby in loading them onto the wagon they would drive to London. She was careful to show no interest in the commotion, staying away from more than a casual peek or two out of the windows as the four men conferred.

When she was back in the kitchen, she looked up as someone strolled in and her heart sank a little when she saw it was Jasper. He crossed to the pantry, rummaging around in it until she finally said, "What is it you need?"

"Apple."

"I put them in yesterday's pie."

He grunted and took himself off, likely to get an early start on the day's drinking and read some sporting news. Junia picked up her dusting cloth and wandered the house until she was able to determine Jem must have gone to town with Dickie.

Between herself, her father, and Major Avondale, they now outnumbered their captors.

Ruthlessly, she pushed down the surge of hope and returned to the kitchen, trying to act as normally as possible as she prepared the trays for the midday meal. She took Major Avondale's to him first, letting Robby lead the way up the stairs and to the door. Just as she stepped inside, she stopped and stamped her foot.

"Oh, drat!"

"What's that, Miss Josephine?"

"I left the teapot in the kitchen." She gave Robby a pleading look, not giving even the barest glance to where Avondale stood next to the hearth. "Would you be a dear and run down to get it for me?"

Robby shuffled his feet, clearly torn. "Dickie said I wasn't to leave you with none of the prisoners."

"You can lock me in," she said brightly. "I'll be safe here until you get back."

Major Avondale caught on quickly and smiled sunnily at Robby. "Miss Josephine had a question for me about, er, Psalm 45. I can answer it for her while she waits."

"There, see?" Junia said. "We will be fine."

"All right, Miss Josephine." Robby shuffled out the door as Major Avondale ostentatiously paged through the shabby Bible in his hand and Junia made a show of setting the tray onto the floor next to his pallet.

They both waited until Robby's footsteps faded down the hall, and then turned to each other. Junia started as she realized how close she stood to him, and he reached out to steady her with a hand on her elbow. They had given him the same lemon-scented soap she used for both herself and the dishes, but it smelled slightly exotic on him, sweetness mixed with a masculine musk.

"They're gone," Junia said, her voice a little breathless in her haste. "It's our best chance."

"I saw them through the window. How many are in the house?"

"Just the two."

Avondale dropped her elbow to pace over to the window and peer out. "It's a long drop. Good chance we break a leg going that way."

"My father has been making a rope in his room," Junia whispered, and Avondale's head snapped to look at her, his gaze intent. Junia could not suppress her little thrill at having him at last treat her like a valued equal, not a schoolgirl.

"So it *is* your father in there. I suspected so."

Footsteps echoed down the hallway, and Avondale returned to where Junia stood, his Bible held open to Psalm 45. She glanced at the first few lines and suppressed a giggle.

"Why did you pick a wedding psalm?" she whispered.

"It was that or the valley of death," he said, and the door opened, Robby carrying the teapot, but a bit shamefaced as Jasper peered around him.

"What's going on?" Jasper said, his words a little slurred. Clearly, he had started the day's drinking as soon as Dickie and Jem were out of sight.

"Nothing at all," Avondale said in a soothing voice. "I was answering a question about psalms."

Jasper continued to scowl as Junia poured the tea into Avondale's empty cup. "This ain't a Sunday school, girl. Get out."

Junia slipped past Robby and Jasper as they re-locked the door and hurried back to the kitchen to fetch her father's tray. She filled his teacup with the pot she still carried and set it down, her hand trembling.

After a deep breath, she hoisted the tray and carried it upstairs to where Jasper and Robby were impatiently waiting next to her father's door.

"I ain't got all day," Jasper grumbled. "Hurry up."

Junia swept her eyes around the room as her father moved the account books from his desk to make room for the tray. With her back still to the door, she formed one word with her lips, not daring to make a sound with the two men watching her.

"Tonight," she mouthed silently, and her father briefly widened his eyes in understanding as she set the tray down on the desk.

JUNIA TOOK a deep breath and did one last inventory. She wore the heavier of her two dresses, with both clean chemises beneath it. She wore both pairs of her clean stockings, one over the other. Her sturdiest shoes were on her feet. Beneath her dress, she'd tied the small purse that held her few pennies and her comb around her waist, uncomfortable but necessary. After one more thought, she tucked the scarf she used to wrap her hair at night and tucked it into her bodice as a fichu. If asked, she could say she felt cold.

She was as prepared as she could be for their escape without alerting Robby or Jasper.

Now she only had to succeed.

One more deep breath, then she removed the wedge from beneath her door and made her way down the short corridor to the kitchen. Robby was already waiting at the table, and she gave him a brief smile.

"I'll fetch your supper, and then you can help me take it upstairs to the others after you've eaten."

He nodded, and watched Junia as she moved around the kitchen, slicing bread and dishing out the stew left bubbling over the banked fire.

With only a little hesitation, she turned her back to him and added a spoonful of dried valerian root to his portion, stirring it in well before handing him the bowl. She then added the same to the bowl meant for Jasper. It would not work as well or as quickly as laudanum, but it might slow the men's reactions enough to give them an advantage.

As Robby worked his way through the stew with his usual methodical greed, Junia loaded up a tray to bring to the dining room.

"He ain't there, Miss Josephine," Robby mumbled through a full mouth.

"Sorry, what?"

"Jasper. He ain't in the dining room. He's outside to guard the pris'ners."

It was the last thing Junia wanted to hear. "Are you supposed to go out there after you eat?"

"That's what Jasper said."

"Oh."

She should have remembered Jasper might not be very bright—after all, he had kidnapped the wrong man—but he was sly, and he knew how to keep someone a prisoner.

"Well, I'll just set this by the stove to keep it warm until you're done and he can come in and eat."

Junia ate her own, unadulterated portion quickly before busying herself with kitchen tasks, trying not to let her agitation show as she reframed her plan. She needed to get her father and Major Avondale out of their rooms and out of the house, while keeping Robby and Jasper inside. And she needed to do it before Dickie and Jem returned at sunset.

She looked over at Robby, who was scraping the bottom of the bowl with his spoon. Sweet, trusting Robby.

He would be far easier to fool than Jasper.

It was too late to worry about every detail. *Go.*

With a decisive gesture, she quickly loaded up the tray with bowls of stew for both of the prisoners and turned to the surprised Robby. "We may as well take the food upstairs now, and then Jasper can eat once we're done."

Obediently, Robby rose to his feet and led the way up the stairs, keys jangling in his hand as they walked, the sound jangling Junia's nerves until she wanted to scream.

He unlocked her father's door first, which only raised her tension, but she thanked him with a smile as he stepped aside to let her in. She set the bowl on the desk, meeting her father's questioning look with a bland smile, and then went back out the door, meekly standing by as Robby re-locked it and then walked the few paces to Major Avondale's door.

It would be her only chance.

As she passed Robby, she deliberately stumbled over the doorjamb, the tray tilting dangerously, and he plucked it out of her hands.

"Oh, thank you," she said. "I don't know how I could be so clumsy. Would you mind setting it down by the hearth for me?"

Robby obeyed, and Junia locked eyes with Major Avondale.

Now.

Almost faster than she could see, Major Avondale leapt at Robby's back while the bigger man was still half-bent over the hearth. Avondale wrapped one arm around Robby's neck and pressed at the other side with his hand, and Robby collapsed almost before he knew what was happening.

Junia stood at the doorway, a hand pressed to her mouth, the sudden violence bringing a wash of nausea to the back of her throat as she pressed away dark memories from her earlier life. "Is he… is he…"

Avondale stepped back, the keys in his hand. "He'll be fine in a few moments, which is why we need to move quickly."

He scooped his cloak from the mattress where it had been serving double duty as a blanket and they pelted from the room, Avondale locking the door to trap Robby inside before letting them into her father's room and slamming it behind them. Her father rose to his feet, rolling down his shirtsleeves and putting his coat on as Avondale locked the door from the inside. The two men nodded to each other.

"Where's Jasper?" Avondale said, and Junia wordlessly pointed to the window. Avondale opened his mouth to say something sharp, glanced at her father, and shook his head instead.

"You should have told me," he hissed.

"There wasn't time. And there's no time now."

Avondale crossed to the window and peered out. Jasper's head was just visible from where he sat on the front steps, smoking a pipe at his leisure, and only a few feet from where they would drop. There was no way to get past without him seeing.

This time Avondale did curse, casting her an apologetic look afterwards.

"Does the window open?" he asked her father.

"I think so. It was painted shut, but I was able to scrape it out."

"If it won't open, we'll break it." Avondale wrapped his hand in the cloak and waited long enough for Junia to begin to fidget.

"What are you waiting—"

A bellow from the next room echoed through the house, bringing Jasper to his feet and darting through the front door. Even as he moved, Avondale first wrenched on the window and then, when it did not budge, punched through it with his fabric-wrapped hand, clearing as much of the glass as possible before laying the doubled cloak across the sill.

In the hallway, they heard Jasper's howl of rage and

banging at first their door and then the other, as Jasper worked to free Robby.

"I'll go first, then Junia, then you, sir," Avondale said.

"My father should go first," Junia protested, but quieted when her father held up his hand.

"He's right. Go, young man."

Avondale vaulted over the windowsill, lowering himself by his hands from the edge of the wall. A crashing sound from the other room sent him dropping to the ground, and Junia leaned out to see he had landed safely. He grinned up at her, and warmth blossomed in her chest despite their danger.

Her father appeared at her elbow and threw his blanket down for Avondale to catch. The sounds from the hallway were louder and angrier as Jasper and Robby threw themselves against the door.

"Go, Junia!"

Swallowing hard, Junia hauled up her skirts and swung her leg over the windowsill. The door burst open just as she succeeded and, with a shriek, she slipped and slid, her father lunging forward to grab her arms and save her from a fall. Despite her frantic grasp, Pappa shook her hands off and let her drop into Avondale's waiting arms.

Even as Junia watched, her father was dragged back into the room by the furious Jasper and Robby. With a last push, her father tipped Avondale's cloak out the window to fall to the ground. Avondale grabbed the cloak and blanket with one hand and Junia with the other, yanking her into a run.

"My father!"

Avondale didn't bother to reply, only dragged her along behind him as Jasper emerged from the house with a howl of rage.

It's only Jasper, she thought. *We can outrun—*

And then she saw the dust of the returning wagon rising only a few hundred yards from them. Dickie squinted from his slouching place beside the driver and then sat up straight with a shout. To Junia's horror, she saw two more rough men in the wagon with Dickie and Jem.

They had brought additional guards.

With no hesitation, Avondale changed direction, pulling Junia through her stumble as they ran into the gathering dusk towards the forest farther out. It would be their only chance to lose their pursuers in the dark and the trees. Junia shook off Avondale's hand, yanked her skirts up past her knees, and ran for her life.

They plunged into the underbrush, and Avondale pulled her down to the ground. He gestured for her to crouch and crawl through, and she nodded her understanding. It would be slower, but leave less of a trail for their pursuers to follow. He handed the blanket to her and gestured for her to tie it around her waist before he began to crawl through the brush.

Ears straining for the muffled sounds of pursuit, Junia followed in Avondale's wake, ducking branches that snapped back as he passed so they would not break and leave evidence of their path. The trailing ends of the blanket continually caught on the branches, frustrating her, but she dared not leave such an obvious trace of their direction behind.

It felt like days, but she knew it could not have been more than an hour before full dark fell and the shouts of pursuit faded away. Avondale kept moving, continuing with a dogged determination Junia had to match, until he stopped abruptly in a small clearing.

Well, not even really a clearing. A spot where the bushes

were slightly lighter, with enough space beneath the branches to form a shelter.

"Stay here," Avondale said in a low voice, and Junia nodded, seating herself on the cold ground while he dropped the cloak next to her and moved into the darkness. Only a few snapping twigs told her he had not abandoned her alone in this strange and chilly country. She sat hunched, draping the cloak around herself and pulling her legs to her chest to stay warm. Every muscle in her body trembled in continuous shivers of shock and fear and cold, and it seemed an eternity before she felt him move close to her again.

His arm wrapped around her, and she stiffened in fear even though she needed the warmth.

❄   4   ❄

Philip cursed himself as Junia stiffened at the unexpected touch, and loosened his grip without letting her go entirely. Whether she admitted it or not, they both needed the extra warmth in the damp chill of the forest.

"You should have let me stay with Pappa," she murmured after a long moment, and he barked a short laugh of disbelief before he could stop himself.

"Leave you behind for them to rape and murder? No. Not ever."

She went silent, which he took as an acknowledgement she knew he was right even if she didn't want to admit it.

A twig snapped nearby and Junia flinched. Reflexively, his arm tightened again to protect and reassure her. It took a conscious effort for him to loosen it.

"What was that?"

"A squirrel. Or a fox. Not heavy enough to be a deer. This is England, not America. We haven't had wolves in three hundred years."

As his eyes adjusted to the dark, he released her to scan the surrounding foliage in the filtered moonlight, carefully pushing at branches and testing the thick fall of dead leaves beneath them. With the addition of a few leafy boughs, it should be sufficient for them to get a little rest.

"We can't risk a fire," he murmured. "They would find us in a heartbeat. I'll break off some extra branches to arrange into a pallet." He paused for a moment, knowing she would dislike his next words. "We'll need to share warmth tonight."

"Is that what men are calling it these days?" she said, her voice a little bitter, and he squeezed her shoulder in gentle reproach.

"My word of honor as a gentleman," he said. "Warmth only. Nothing more." The thought of *something more* with her made heat surge up his spine, but he loosened his hold and dropped his arm.

She turned her head to look at him for a long time as if judging his honesty, her sharp gaze penetrating the gloom under the shrubbery. At last, she nodded. "All right, then. Your word of honor."

He crept out from under their cover to locate a few leafy branches that seemed resilient enough to cushion them from the ground. Breaking them off without the aid of his penknife was more difficult than he thought, but eventually he crawled back into their hideaway in triumph. Junia shifted aside to allow him to lay the branches down.

He arranged the threadbare blanket on top of the branches, testing for any sharp edges that poked through, and then extended his hand to her. After a slight hesitation, she took it and allowed him to adjust the cloak around them both before wrapping his arm around her shoulders to snug her against his side. She sat stiffly for a long time, until finally, with a sigh, she allowed herself to relax a little.

Now that they were alone in the dark together, he was more aware than ever that she was a full-grown woman, but he would not—*could* not—betray her trust. They only had each other to rely on while they made their way to London, and he would never forgive himself if she were put into further danger because of his inability to control himself.

He needed to remember he was an officer. And a gentleman. No matter how deliciously she smelled of lemon, fresh-baked bread, and herself.

"Why did they kidnap you?"

He pushed his lustful thoughts away, and kept his voice as low as hers. "They thought I was my brother, Peter. It's an honest mistake, of a sort. We are twins, after all."

"Twins? Identical?"

"Yes. The despair of our mother, and of every schoolmaster we encountered."

"And he's really a minister?"

"At the moment, he's on trial as a curate at St. Luke's in Islington. He was, er, asked to leave his last parish when he disagreed with the vicar about how to best minister to their poor, so he's a bit at loose ends right now."

"Tell me about him," she said, and her head dropped onto his shoulder. His arm tightened around her, holding her closer.

For warmth. Of course.

~

Junia listened with half an ear as Avondale spoke, drained from their escape. She had to admit it was nice to sit with him like this in the dark and the chill, almost like their own private little world. Moonlight filtered through the leaves, and she could hear night birds and insects begin to call around them. They almost sounded like the waves on board ship, when they had walked on deck together with a score of sailors as chaperones.

She started from her half-drowse when he shook her shoulder. "What?"

He covered her mouth. "Sound carries at night," he said, his lips only a breath away from her ear, and she shivered. "We should both try to sleep."

He made her shift so he could straighten the blanket on the ground and then lay on his side, gesturing for her to lay in front of him as he arranged the cloak over them.

Junia frowned. "Word of honor?"

She could see his smile flash out in the filtered moonlight. "Word of honor."

Cautiously, she lay down on her side and his arm went around her waist, pulling her back against his front. She stiffened, a flash of remembered panic going through her, but she slowly relaxed as he made no other move, merely pillowing his head on his arm with a sigh.

When she followed suit by pillowing her head on her own arm, he murmured in her ear, "Then there was the time Peter decided fox hunting was cruel—which it is—but his method of keeping the hunters from the foxes was to hide leftover bits of chicken all around the hunting ground, only some of the bits were well past their prime…"

With his warmth surrounding her and his voice vibrating

behind her back, Junia soon found herself drifting off into a light doze.

PHILIP LET his voice trail off as he felt her relax against him and her breathing fall into a regular pattern. The tension of knowing they were being hunted would be enough to keep him alert during the night, though the danger was reduced with every hour that passed. Dickie and the rest of his gang were city dwellers who would not be comfortable beating through the forest at night.

Memories of pursuit raised a vision in his mind's eye of the first time he had seen Junia, a frightened, half-starved waif clinging to her younger sister's waist as sailors hauled them aboard the British warship.

"There!" She had grabbed Philip's sleeve, her grip surprisingly strong for someone who appeared so frail, and pointed. "My parents. You must help them!"

Philip raised his spyglass and spotted the tiny craft being roiled by the ocean. An older man and woman were aboard it, boxes piled around them as the man rowed and the woman steered towards the warship. Another boat rowed in pursuit, closing the distance until a warning shot from one of the British riflemen pierced the water in front of them and caused them to veer away. American curses rang out across the water as they abandoned the hunt.

He had barked out orders for a craft to be launched for the rescue as a sailor's wife rushed up from the bottom of the ship to take the girls in hand. Junia had refused to let herself be led away with her sister. She'd stood shivering at the railing until, at last, her parents were safely on board, first her mother and then her father.

Her father had looked around the deck and finally settled on Philip as the officer in charge. Caius Reynolds was a balding man of middle height, soaked to the skin, dressed in threadbare clothes, but his inherent dignity demanded respect. He walked to Philip and bowed.

"We's claiming asylum from slavery."

Philip had bowed in return. "Welcome aboard, sir."

Junia had watched the little drama from her place by the railing with her mother's protective arm around her. When Philip looked at her, a shy but radiant smile had blossomed across her face before she buried her face in her mother's shoulder and finally allowed herself to be led belowdecks.

The ship had returned to England with ninety-seven individuals who had escaped slavery, including Junia's family. That war had brought many frustrations and an eventual loss to British prestige, but escorting those people to freedom in England was a wartime action Philip could look back on with pride.

He looked down at Junia through the darkness and tightened his own arm around her. He had never quite been able to forget her, though his code as a gentleman and an officer had prevented him from treating her as anything more than an honored guest on board the ship.

Over the past four years, she had blossomed from a seventeen-year-old girl into a full-grown woman, but his word of honor still kept him from her. Only a scoundrel would take advantage of a woman in her position, no matter how strongly his unruly body and even more unruly emotions urged him to.

He closed his eyes and tried to rest. Knowing Junia was warm and safe in his arms helped calm his mind enough to doze off.

JUNIA WOKE SLOWLY, wrapped in drowsy warmth. The mattress beneath her was cozy and firm, much better than the thin pallet she had been sleeping on for weeks, though it had a few peculiar lumps. She allowed herself to drift along the edge of sleep, knowing a return to full consciousness would mean having to leave this luxurious feeling of contentment and safety behind.

The pillow supporting her back shifted, and she realized it must be an arm.

Major Avondale's arm.

The thought should have been alarming, but his touch was protective, comforting, not lustful. She peered through her eyelashes and the first light of dawn showed they had shifted in the night so she lay with her head pillowed on his shoulder, half-laying on him as he cradled her with one arm, the other pillowing his own head. His face was a little turned away from her, and she took a moment to admire his firm profile in the gathering light. Fresh stubble had formed on his clean-shaven cheeks overnight, blurring the precise lines of his sidewhiskers.

Damp cold seeped up from the ground and through the blanket they lay on, but Junia did not want to move. She had never woken up in a man's arms before. She didn't want to spoil the moment.

Inevitably, a loud cheep from a bird in the trees overhead

roused him. His arm tightened around her for a moment and she melted into him, still relaxed with sleep. He turned his head and smiled at her.

"Are you ready to start heading to London?"

Junia pulled away and sat up, abruptly returned to reality. "London? What about my father?"

Avondale sighed and sat up as well, running a hand through his wildly disordered hair. "What do you think you and I can do against six armed men, Junia? We must go to London and get reinforcements."

She wanted to argue, but reluctantly nodded her agreement. She hated knowing he was right.

He maneuvered to the largest gap in the branches and got to his feet, stretching against the aches of sleeping on the ground, and Junia was suddenly aware of her own aches. She stumbled to her feet and stretched as well, watching him as he turned around the tiny clearing.

"Are we north or south of London?"

"North," she said. "It might be northeast."

He nodded, and looked at her curiously. "How did you find him?"

Junia turned away, shaking out her skirts. "I saw them take him. They grabbed him off the street." She shuddered with the remembered terror of seeing her father dragged away and pushed into a carriage that abruptly drove away. In a matter of moments, she had been abandoned on the pavement, standing helpless with her weeping sister clinging to her as their father vanished around a corner.

"But *how* did you find them?"

"I recognized the horse and carriage," she said. "It was one we had hired ourselves, from time to time. I was able to ask at the livery stable and then make my plan for when they returned it."

"Quick thinking on your part," he said.

Junia tossed her head. "I can think on occasion."

"I meant no insult, Miss Reynolds. You are a very clever woman."

"And yet my father is still held prisoner."

"We will remedy that as soon as possible. You have my word on it."

"You give me your word often, my lord. How do I know you will keep it?"

He looked at her steadily, and the anger in her ebbed a little, knowing it was not him she was angry with.

"You will need to trust me," he said, "as I will trust you to help us get back to London so we can save your father."

She had no other choice, really.

He raked her with a critical glance. "Would you be able to untie your headwrap and wear it more like a kerchief?"

Her hand flew to the tucked-in ends. She had tied it on the night before to prevent her hair from becoming hopelessly matted while sleeping rough, thankful she had not lost it in their flight.

"Yes, I think so. Why?"

"They'll be looking for us, and your complexion is unusual enough in the countryside that people might notice you more than they would in London. If you can conceal your face from casual passers-by, it might confuse our pursuers a little longer."

"All right." Reluctantly, she unwound the patterned cloth and folded it into a triangle that she draped over her head and tied beneath her chin, shading her face with the edges.

He nodded in approval. She held her breath as he raised his hand to her temple and carefully tucked a wayward cluster of curls under the cloth, his fingertips lingering on her skin for a moment before he withdrew his hand and stepped back.

"If we head straight to the main road, they'll spot us immediately," he said. "I'm afraid we'll have to go across the fields and come to it roundabout. I don't suppose you brought any food."

"I'm sorry, no," she said, thinking of the freshly made loaf of bread she'd abandoned yesterday. "I couldn't figure out how to carry it without alerting Jasper and Robby. I have a few pence with me, though."

"All right. Let's get started. Leave the blanket, but bring the cloak."

The sun was only just barely over the horizon, mist rising from the ground as the air began to warm. Avondale led her cross-country, helping her over stiles and low stone walls when they came to them. The cloak swirled around her ankles and caught at brambles until she took it off in exasperation and folded it over her arm instead.

"Did you walk from London?" he asked.

"Not all the way. I was able to take a hansom to the edge of the city, and then found several rides along the way."

"It seemed to take several hours when they kidnapped me."

"It was at least four hours by cart, and that was starting from a market on the north end of the city."

Avondale frowned, and she could see him calculating the distance in his head. "We're further out than I realized."

"Do you... do you think they'll find us?"

"My dear Miss Reynolds," he said, "if I was able to avoid

being captured by Napoleon's troops while I was on the Peninsula, I feel confident I can evade a few thugs in my own country."

Junia was less confident, but she nodded and fell into step beside him. As they walked, he scanned and rescanned the area, sometimes turning and walking backwards a few steps to check for pursuit from behind.

After about an hour, he paused and pointed to a small speck nestled among some trees on the horizon. "You see that cottage?"

She squinted. If she looked hard, she thought she could see a tiny curl of smoke rising from the speck. "Yes, I think so."

"I think we need to go beg some bread, get under cover for a short while. We're too exposed out here."

"We don't have to beg. I have my wages. I think it's twelve pence—that makes a shilling?"

"Let's save that until we have need of it. For the time being, we can trade chores for some food."

Junia still did not like the sound of it, but he spoke so casually that it must be a common thing to do in the countryside. They turned their steps towards the cottage, which slowly came into focus as a tiny stone house with a thin plume of smoke coming from the chimney. An old woman sat in the front yard with a pipe and watched them approach.

Avondale stopped a good distance away and bowed to her. "Good morning, madam."

"Morning," she said warily.

"My… wife and I are traveling but find ourselves short on coin. Would there be a few chores around the cottage we could do in exchange for some food?"

Junia saw the woman glance at her, so she untied her kerchief to show her face better and smiled at her. "We would be very grateful if you could."

The old woman puffed meditatively on her pipe as she looked them over. "I'll make a bargain with ye. Nancy's gone off to visit her ailing ma, and I twisted me ankle last night. Snowdrop's been agitatin' to be milked for an hour now, and I can't get to the shed to let her out or bend to milk her. Take care of her, and I'll have some cheese and bread for you after."

"It's a bargain, madam," Avondale said before Junia could stop him, and she widened her eyes to try and signal him. She had no idea how to milk a cow, and she was fairly certain he didn't either.

The shed was not more than a few yards away, and the animal noises coming from inside it grew more urgent as they approached. Avondale gestured for Junia to precede him into the shed, where she looked down at the animal inside the stall.

"I don't think that's a cow."

"No," Avondale said. "That's a goat. Do you know how to milk a goat?"

Junia shook her head, horrified. "I grew up at the city house. We bought our milk at the market."

Avondale sighed and ran a hand through his hair. "I milked a cow once, when I was a lad. Father thought we ought to understand at least some of the workings of the tenant farmers."

"Then you should do it," she said firmly. "I don't have the least idea how."

Junia did not like the look of the animal at all, with its

strangely slitted eyes and rough coat, but its bleats *were* rather piteous. She sighed and opened the door to its stall.

The goat bolted past both of them and out into the yard. He cursed and they ran to chase it, only to discover it already standing on a peculiar low platform, its nose stuck into an attached box. It raised its head and bleated at them again, this time sounding annoyed.

"You need to put some clean hay in there," the old woman shouted over from her seat in the yard, her rough voice filled with glee at their predicament. "Keeps her calm while you work."

Muttering, Avondale went back into the shed and came out with an armload of hay he dumped into the box. The goat immediately stuck its head in and began chomping away.

Junia placed the bucket the woman had given them onto the platform and peered under the goat's body. The poor thing's udder did appear quite swollen.

Avondale heaved a heavy sigh. "Are you really going to make me do this?"

"Yes," Junia said, trying to prevent her lips from twitching into a grin.

He stepped forward and bent to take one teat into his hand. He gave it a tentative tug, and the goat bleated and stepped aside.

"You'll have to hold her back legs, missy," the old woman shouted. "Don't be afraid to be firm with her."

Avondale grinned, and for a moment Junia considered changing her mind about the milking. She took another look at the bulging udder and shuddered. She couldn't. She just couldn't.

With a sigh of resignation, she moved into position and put her hands around the goat's lower legs to hold her steady. The goat shifted and protested a bit, but soon returned to her breakfast.

Avondale squatted to examine the goat's teats.

"Don't be shy, young man. Squeeze from the top of the udder and give her teat a little tug. You'll know the motion in a moment."

To her surprise, Junia saw a dark flush—of embarrassment?—climb up Avondale's cheeks. Then he started the motion as directed, and Junia could feel her own embarrassed flush begin. It was... suggestive, that stroking motion, but it seemed effective because milk began spurting out into the pail.

Avondale's blush only deepened, but he continued doggedly as Junia held the goat steady, switching from one teat to the other according to the shouted instructions until he found the rhythm. Junia found herself mesmerized by the motions, watching his strong hands working on the animal, his movements seeming somehow familiar in a primal way. She found herself holding her breath until at last the flow of milk slowed and stopped, and Avondale stood up from his crouch.

He looked at her, and she knew he had been feeling the same primal connection to his rhythmic motions.

Oh. This *is what it feels like to desire someone.*

"You can let go of her now, missy. She's all done."

Startled, Junia let go of the goat, who continued eating, and stepped away from the platform. Avondale picked up the bucket and they walked to where their hostess sat.

"Thankee kindly, and Snowdrop thanks ye, too. Let me

lean on your arm a bit, missy, while your man brings the milk."

Once inside, the woman instructed Avondale on how to strain the milk while Junia quietly moved around the small kitchen, rinsing her hands under the kitchen pump and cleaning the dishes she found there.

"Bread and cheese is in the pantry. May as well cut us all a slice of pie while you're in there, too."

The pie proved to be gooseberry, and Junia brought it out with the rest of the food, along with a pitcher of small beer. Avondale had washed his own hands and settled their hostess into a chair next to the banked fire. Junia brought a plate to her, along with a mug of beer, and set it on a small table next to her chair. She arranged a small footstool to prop her sore ankle onto, and the older woman sighed with relief before she started to eat.

Junia joined Avondale at the battered kitchen table, where he had served each of them a portion of the meal. The cheese was goat cheese, of course, tangy and earthy, more delicious than Junia expected and soft enough to spread. The bread was only a day old, a hearty brown loaf of a type Junia guessed Avondale had not seen since his army days, given the way he frowned skeptically at it before taking a bite, and then another, with evident enjoyment.

Having Avondale sitting across from her in his rolled-up shirtsleeves, dark curls tousled, was more intimate than Junia could have believed. She could almost dream they were married, working together on their farm before retiring for the evening...

She caught Avondale's gaze across the table and immediately redirected her eyes to her plate. Fortunately, he would not be able to see her flush of confusion in the dimly-lit room.

Their hostess gave out a loud sigh and a small belch as she set down the empty plate that had held her slice of pie. "Where are ye off to after this?"

"London," Avondale said, turning his gaze away from Junia.

"Never been there. It's a full twenty miles away, at the least."

"Which way to the main road from here?"

"Eh, if you cut across going southwest, you'll reach it. I'll point you when you're ready."

"Is there anything more we can do for you before we go?" Junia asked. "I'll clean the dishes, of course, but anything else?"

"That's right kind of you, missy. There's a thing or two, if you don't mind."

Junia followed her instructions to bring food from the pantry to make it more accessible until Nancy returned the next day, safely covered from mice and other pests. Avondale was sent up to the attic to locate a crutch left there by the woman's late husband while Junia tidied and swept after their meal. At their hostess's insistence, Junia wrapped some bread and firm cheese in a clean rag to take with them. After a short discussion with Avondale, Junia shyly offered her the cloak as partial payment for her assistance, which she accepted.

"I must say, I've enjoyed the comp'ny, too," she said. "Stop on by next time you're around."

Avondale laughed and took the old woman's hand to bow over it. "Thank you for your hospitality, madam."

She cast a shrewd look up at him. "And don't tell none I've seen you, eh?"

"No," he said. "But I promise you we're not thieves."

She waved an airy hand. "You'd've been able to murder me a dozen times over by now if that was your aim. But you're not that kind." She pointed across the fields to a small hill. "Head that way. Village is behind that hill, then go south to the main road."

Impulsively, Junia leaned down and kissed the old woman's cheek. "Thank you."

The woman pulled her close and whispered in her ear, "Hang onto that man of yours, missy. He's a game one."

Junia pulled back, choked on her denial, and just smiled.

❀　5　❀

As they walked in the direction of the village, Junia saw Avondale frown at the sky.

"What is it?"

"Rain clouds," he said. "They're heading straight towards us." He pointed to where dark clouds gathered on the horizon, and she feared he was right about their direction.

"What should we do?"

"Keep heading towards the village. I don't want to get caught out in the rain if we can avoid it."

After a long stretch of walking, Avondale spoke again. "Why did they abduct your father?"

"We don't know."

"You don't know?"

Junia puffed out a breath. "He's making changes to the accounting books they bring him, but the changes have to add up on each page, and be done in a way that ends with a correct total, which they provide to him on a sheet of paper. He could work through them more quickly, but he's unwilling to do it until he knows what they're planning to do with him once he's done."

Philip frowned. "We need to get him out of there as soon as we can find reinforcements. We don't know what they'll do when he finishes whatever task it is they've set for him."

She stumbled, and he put his arm around her to prevent her from falling. "It's all right. Don't fret, angel. We'll get him out."

Junia let herself lean against him just a little, and his arm tightened. She felt safe with him, safer than she had felt in weeks. Months. Years.

Dangerously safe.

She straightened her posture and his arm fell away.

The road sank down into a small lane lined by hedges and trees. Avondale looked around it, a slight frown on his face.

"What is it?"

"I don't like it. Feels like an ambush point."

His unease put her on edge as well, and their steps slowed as he scanned the hedges until he found a break just large enough for them to squeeze through. She looked into the small space with distaste.

"Really?"

"Humor me." He gave her arm a small, encouraging push. She sighed and followed his direction, squeezing through the narrow space until they passed through to a thick stand of birch trees just behind the hedge. He helped her maneuver between them until they stood on a small ridge above the lane that had been invisible from the ground.

Silently, he pointed to a spot just past where the lane rose again. She could see dust settling, as though horses or a cart had passed through.

He leaned down to say quietly, "Come this way."

As they edged their way through the trees, a cart emerged into view, and they froze, half-concealed by the branches. Jasper and Robby sat together on the driver's seat, Jasper guiding the horse as Robby kept watch.

"That shepherd said he saw them heading this way," Jasper grumbled. "Should have known not to trust him."

Robby's head stopped scanning, and for a moment, he met Junia's eyes. He saw her. She knew he did.

Then he turned his head to the other side of the road and the cart continued on in the opposite direction.

As the sound of its wheels faded away, Junia sagged against Avondale, and he pulled her against his side, his arm around her waist.

"He saw you."

"I know."

Avondale was silent for a long moment. "He must have liked your cooking."

Junia snorted, then giggled, then laughed out loud while he grinned down at her. "That's a terrible joke."

"It's not terrible if it makes you laugh."

The sudden seriousness in his eyes made her cast hers down in confusion. Of its own volition, her hand crept up the lapel of his coat, fingers curling under until she could feel the heat of his body seeping through the fabric. His arm tightened around her and she yielded, pressing herself against him and resting her head on his shoulder for a long moment before she tilted her face up to his.

He was going to kiss her. And she wanted him to.

He hesitated for a long moment, his eyes searching hers, until she gave his lapel a little tug to bring him closer. With a groan, he tipped his head and brushed her lips with his once, then again, and again, staying a little longer each time until their mouths met and melded for a long moment.

He raised his head, and she smiled at him, knowing she was starry-eyed.

"Avondale."

He dipped his head again. "Call me Philip," he murmured, his lips only a breath away from hers.

"Philip."

He rewarded her with another kiss, one that sent warmth rushing all the way from her head to her toes and back again until she was clinging to him.

A sudden blast of damp wind buffeted them, and with a laugh and a shake of his head, he stepped back.

"We need to get on to the village before the rain comes."

Junia's head was still spinning from the kiss, so she only nodded and followed his lead as they threaded their way through the trees parallel to the road.

❦   6   ❦

The sky grew darker and grimmer as they walked, mist mixing with raindrops which became more and more frequent. At last, the foggy shapes of the village came into view.

"I think the inn is that building on the end," Philip said.

"Oh." Junia stopped walking and frowned at the lights glimmering through the gathering fog. "Should we keep going?"

"By no means," Philip said. "We'll stop there for the night."

"What?"

He resumed walking with the determined steps of a man who had spotted a refuge, and she hurried after him.

"We can't stop at an inn."

"Why not?" he said.

"They almost just found us. It's the first place they'll look."

"They'll be looking for us in hedgerows and barns. They assume we don't have any money."

"We don't have any money, at least not enough for an inn. Do we?"

He turned his head to grin at her, and continued walking. She followed behind, not sure if she should be angry or hopeful.

As they came to a small bridge across a creek—no, they called it a brook here—Philip paused to sit on the edge and turn up the bottom of his boot.

To Junia's astonishment, he twisted the heel to reveal a short stack of four or five gold sovereigns that jingled in his hand. He replaced the heel and put the coins into his waistcoat pocket before returning to his feet. The rain was coming down in earnest now, streaming around them, and she adjusted the scarf that had shielded her face to better cover her hair.

"We need to play our parts well," he said, "to avoid any awkward questions."

"And what is my part, may I ask?"

He shrugged off his coat and put it around her shoulders. "My wife, of course, who is shaken up by our carriage accident and needs a safe place to rest for the night."

Junia couldn't help her little shiver as the warmth from his body surrounded her, carried by the wool of his coat. She inhaled as discreetly as she could, enjoying his scent as it rose around her.

"Lean on me," he said, and she was not reluctant to obey him. He put his arm around her, and she allowed herself to dream a little. To dream she really was his beloved wife, that he was concerned for her safety after their accident, that his head bent over hers and his arm circled her waist because he cared for her.

He pushed open the door of the inn and Junia blinked at the noise and light inside, her eyes taking a moment to adjust after their walk in the fog. Instinctively, she moved closer to him, as timid as the part she was playing, and he took a moment to give her a reassuring squeeze before he shouted for the innkeeper.

A rotund little man hurried over, rubbing his hands on his apron as he took in Philip's fine linen shirt and the quality of the superfine wool of his coat. "Yes, milord! How can we help you?"

"My wife and I suffered a carriage accident," Philip said, and Junia shrank against him under the innkeeper's sharp gaze. "We require a room for the night."

"Certainly, milord. Right this way."

Junia squeaked as Philip scooped her up into his arms, cradling her against his chest. She flung her arms around his neck to keep her balance.

"It's all right, my dove," he said, a wicked gleam in his eye. "Only a few more minutes and we'll be alone again."

She longed to give his neck a sharp pinch, but feared he would drop her retaliation, so she only glared at him before dropping her head onto his shoulder. The landlord opened a door at the top of the stairs and Philip stepped through. Over his shoulder, Junia could see a curious maidservant follow them in, her eyes widening as she registered the color of Junia's skin before Junia ducked her head.

"Build up the fire," Philip commanded in his most aristocratic tones. "My wife is lately arrived from Jamaica and is not accustomed to our damp climate."

"Yes, milord!" the maidservant said, her prompt actions filled with a new respect. Junia could see news of the fabulously wealthy mixed-race Jamaican heiresses arriving in London and Edinburgh had reached even this small village, and the maid was now more interested in a possible tip than in the color of Junia's skin.

He crossed to the bed and set Junia down on it, and she lay back with a sigh. It was certainly more comfortable than sleeping in the woods again.

Philip flashed a golden guinea from his waistcoat pocket, and suddenly the room was filled with a flurry of activity as servants scurried back and forth, bringing food and hot water for washing as Philip directed them all.

Then he closed the door behind the last curtseying maidservant, and they were alone together.

Junia lay out the meal, dividing the meat pie between the two of them and pouring ale from the pitcher. Without further conversation, she dove in, hoping her greed would not disgust him but unable to be more ladylike after a long day of walking with nothing more than bread and cheese to sustain her. She glanced up to see he was equally absorbed in his food, eventually putting his fork down with a satisfied sigh. She took one last sip from her tankard and sighed herself, replete. They both drowsed in their chairs by the fire, their most urgent bodily needs satisfied.

Which made Junia aware of a new tension in the room. Now that they had food and safety and warmth, the knowledge they were alone—and would be alone all night— was making her wonder what she would do if he kissed her again.

She was not sure of the answer.

He cleared his throat and gestured to the screen in the corner. "I'll go down for a pint while you wash."

"Thank you," Junia said, knowing her voice shook a little.

He crossed to her chair and bent to brush a chaste kiss on her lips before grinning at her. "It's a respectable inn, and I'll be right downstairs. But I'll lock the door when I go, just in case."

She looked up at him, her lips tingling from just that casual touch. "All right."

As soon as the key turned in the lock, Junia leapt to the washbasin behind a screen in the corner. She made use of the chamber pot before stripping down to wash from the basin. A full bath would need to wait until she was home in London, but having soap and hot wash water was heavenly. She shook out the cleaner of her two shifts, pulled it on, and dove under the covers of the bed, her heart pounding. While she waited, she did her best to untangle some of the mats from her hair. That, too, might have to wait until she could have her mother's or Zillah's help in London.

The key turned in the lock, and she pulled the quilt up to her neck as the door opened and Philip entered. He retrieved the kettle that had been set next to the hearth and went behind the screen to pour fresh hot water into the basin, but came back looking a little grim.

He sat on the edge of the bed and she stared at him, frozen.

"Junia."

"Yes?"

"If it would make you more comfortable…" He trailed off and then took a deep breath. "If it would make you more comfortable, I could sleep on the floor."

"Oh."

Look into your heart, she knew her mother would say.

She took a deep breath and looked.

Her mother would likely not approve, but her mother was not here, and Junia knew what she wanted.

She looked at Philip, who was watching her, his face still solemn.

"You don't have to sleep on the floor," she said.

He blinked, as if surprised, and then a grin broke across his face. "Really?"

"Really." Daring greatly, she put a hand up to his cheek and leaned towards him. He leaned in the rest of the distance, kissing her softly until she demanded more, and he pulled away with a chuckle.

"Let me wash first."

"All right," she said, unable to stop smiling. She knew with her head he could never marry her, had always known that, even in her girlish daydreams. There were too many barriers between them. But her heart could not resist the opportunity to have this one night with him, even if it could never lead to anything more.

She would take what he offered tonight and worry about the consequences tomorrow.

PHILIP WASHED as quickly as he could, trying to leash his eagerness. He could scarcely believe he had found her again, much less that she was waiting for him in a warm, cozy bed. The swiftness of events dizzied him, but he had no intention of losing this unexpected chance, even if it changed nothing on the morrow.

He frowned at his shirt, which had become more than a

little overripe during his weeklong captivity. Serving on the Peninsula had taught him a quick soak in soapy water followed by a rinse would at least reduce the worst of the smell, especially if he could spread it on the hearth to dry. After a small hesitation, he pulled his breeches back on and walked around the edge of the screen, wet shirt in hand.

Junia was sitting up in bed, the covers clutched to her shoulders, and her eyes widened as she saw him shirtless, a blush giving her dark cheeks a rosy glow even in the dim light of the room.

He chuckled. "Give me a moment, angel, and you can look your fill."

He spread the shirt on the flagstones of the hearth, far enough away to avoid any sparks but close enough to get a little heat to dry it. He turned to see Junia still watching him, her lips a little parted as though she was having trouble catching her breath. Unable to resist, he sauntered towards her, enjoying how much she seemed to enjoy looking at him. Leaving his breeches on, he turned up the covers and slid underneath as she slid over. He rolled to his side and propped himself up on his elbow, grinning at her. She followed suit, though she kept her eyes downcast.

He put a finger under her chin and tilted her face up to his. "Hello."

"Hello," she said, her voice breathless, and he kissed her, dampening her lips with his, grazing her bottom lip with his teeth before teasing it with his tongue. To his delight, she responded in kind, following his lead until he rolled over on top of her, luxuriating in the feeling of her soft body beneath his.

He bent to kiss her again… but she didn't respond.

Frowning, he opened his eyes to see hers were squeezed closed, her expression tense. "Junia?"

She opened her eyes, but they were no longer filled with passion. It was something closer to panic. "I... I'm all right."

Philip frowned and rolled to the side, removing his weight from her. "What's wrong?"

"Nothing. I'm fine." The smile on her face was clearly false, and she tensed a little more when he reached out to stroke down her arm.

He sighed and rolled onto his back, tugging her to lie against his bare chest, her head pillowed on his shoulder. She resisted for a moment before cuddling against him with a sigh.

Philip had been to war, and he knew much of slavery. He had a good idea why Junia had reacted the way she had, but he did not want to push her into any confidences she was not comfortable making. So instead they lay together for long minutes as he gently stroked her back and arms, soothing her into relaxation.

At last, she looked up at him. "I'm sorry."

"Don't be." He hesitated, not sure he wanted to know the truth, but also unwilling to ignore what had happened just now. "Do you want to tell me about it?"

She ducked her head back down and burrowed her face against his naked chest. "No. Yes. No."

"All right." He continued with his undemanding caresses, willing to be as patient as he needed to be. When at last she began to speak, her voice was so low he had to bend his head to hear her, and the English accent she had adopted dropped away to her original, American one.

"The young master, he come home for Miss Patsy's debut. We all knew to avoid him, but he caught me in her dressing room while the mistress and her daughters was out paying calls and I was doing the pressing."

Junia drew in a long, shuddering breath, and Philip was careful to keep his touch gentle. "He pushed a pillow over my face, and he put all his weight on me so I couldn't scream, I couldn't get a breath, I thought he was going to smother me…"

She stopped on a choked sob that tore at his heart. Her hand curved around his shoulder to press herself against him, seeking comfort with an unspoken trust that made his heart swell even as he kept his touch light and reassuring.

"When he finished, he said a bag of bones like me wasn't even worth the ride. I ate as little as I could after that, to keep him away."

"Then what happened?"

"Miss Patsy beat me," Junia said matter-of-factly. "For corrupting her brother. And the mistress was angry, too. There wasn't no one else she could train up to be the lady's maid for her girls, and if I fell pregnant, it would ruin Miss Ellen's debut, too. But Mama gave me cotton bark tea to bring on my flowers so it wouldn't happen."

One more racking breath, and he felt her tension begin to ebb. "That was when Pappa decided we should escape instead of saving up to buy our freedom. He knew it would only get worse when Zillah started working abovestairs like me."

Philip pressed his face into the puff of her hair, pushing down the rage that threatened to claw free. He could vent it later, when he was at Gentleman Jackson's or on the hunting field. He could not, *would* not burden her with his own emotions at this moment.

She tilted her head back to look into his eyes, her face solemn. "Do you think differently about me now?"

"I think," he said, "you are the most courageous woman I have ever met, to come through all you have and not be broken by it."

A shy smile crossed her face. "You only say that because you don't know my mama."

He cupped her face in his hands and kissed her, and the sweet fire of her response now that her burden had been shared nearly made him weep.

"I still want to… to be with you," she said, and the trepidation in her beautiful eyes made his heart wrench even as his body tightened at her willingness.

And then an idea sparked, and he let a rakish smile spread across his face as he turned onto his side again and propped his head up on his hand.

"Tell me, angel," he said. "Do you ever touch yourself?"

Her jaw dropped open. "Really, Philip!"

His grin grew wider. He could feel the blush radiating from her skin as she ducked her face into his shoulder.

It wasn't a no.

He dipped his head to brush his lips against her ear, and then the little hollow beneath it.

"Show me."

Junia shook her head, keeping her face hidden. "I can't."

He let his lips drift down to the exposed curve of her neck and felt her shiver. "I want to know how to please you, and you know that better than anyone can. Show me."

He felt her take in a deep breath and release it.

And then she rolled to her back and parted her legs, her face turned away from him.

"I can't look at you while I do it," she whispered, and he brushed another kiss across her bare shoulder.

"Don't worry about it, angel."

He leaned back to watch her, memorizing the contrast between the rich brown of her limbs and the stark white of the sheets, the way the neckline of her chemise dipped towards her half-bared breasts as her hand tentatively began to move, her breath quickening as she pleasured herself.

He watched for as long as he could stand it, almost relishing how his hands itched to smooth over her skin and feel the slight sheen of sweat that was beginning to form. Then he leaned forward to kiss his way from her shoulder back to her ear, feeling her breath catch.

"May I kiss you, Junia?"

She nodded and turned her head toward him. He brushed his lips against hers, gently at first, deepening the kiss by degrees until she arched up to him, tongue meeting and playing with his.

Careful to keep his weight off her, he leaned a little away. "May I kiss you other places?"

A puzzled frown formed between her brows. "Where?"

He let his mouth slide down her neck to the top slopes of her breasts. "I could start here."

She nodded, her eyes wide, and he nudged the chemise lower to bare her breasts to his view. She closed her eyes as his mouth moved lower, her breath coming fast, and he licked across one deep brown nipple, feeling it harden under his tongue as her back arched.

"How does that feel, Junia?" he purred.

"I... good. It feels... good."

"Do you want me to do it again?"

"Yes. *Yes*."

He swirled his tongue, bringing her nipple up hard and tight. Lightly, he skimmed his hand along her side, down to her hip, and hovered just above her belly. Her eyes fluttered open.

"May I touch you, Junia?" His hand drifted closer to where she used hers to pleasure herself. He could feel the moisture and the heat, and he swallowed hard as she slowly nodded.

She tensed a little as his fingers stroked down the length of her thigh before caressing their way up, gently urging her legs further apart. He leaned down and kissed the small frown between her eyebrows before he kissed her lips.

"Trust me," he said. She nodded hesitantly, and he let his finger brush against the moist opening of her body, gently at first, then more purposefully as he found the entrance and slid his fingertip inside.

She gasped, and he looked up at her sharply. "Does it hurt?"

"No."

He slid it in further, feeling her inner muscles yield to the gentle pressure, watching her face as she closed her eyes.

This was how she would feel around his cock, tight and slick and hot, and he moved his finger the way he hoped to move inside her, stroking deep and retreating, imitating her rhythm until her hips arched upward to follow his motion even as her own hand continued to move, faster and faster.

He slid a second finger in, gently stretching her, feeling her inner muscles clench around him until she cried out and he felt her orgasm surrounding him, drawing him in until she shuddered one last time and relaxed.

He slid his hand away and watched her for a long moment, flushed and beautiful, until at last she turned her head towards him and opened her eyes. He bent to kiss her.

"Still embarrassed?"

"Yes. But—"

Her hand slid behind his head and pulled his mouth down to hers in a kiss so luscious he feared he would lose control right there.

She loosened her grip just enough to let him pull back a few inches. "I still want more."

He stripped off his breeches under the covers and rolled atop her again. Without her conscious volition, her body froze. He slid back to the side, and tears of frustration rose in her eyes.

"I'm sorry."

"It's not your fault." He kissed her lightly. "Besides, there's more than one way to do this."

Puzzled, she watched as he sat up with his back against the headboard before guiding her to sit up as well. She took a moment to admire him, broad shoulders seeming to take up the whole space. She extended a hand to comb through the thick pelt of hair on his chest, stroking across and then down to where it narrowed as if to point to his...

"Oh, my," she said, and glanced up to see he was watching her, his expression avid.

"Do whatever feels right for you, angel," he said. "I can take it."

She swallowed and let her hand stray down the hard line of his stomach until she hovered just above... it.

"I don't know what to call it," she said, knowing her voice was a little plaintive, and he laughed a rough laugh.

"It doesn't have a proper name, unless you want to give it one. I just call it my cock."

Her hand reached out of its own accord, and she glanced up at him. He nodded, his gaze burning into hers, and she took a deep breath and let her fingers curl around it.

It was a surprise how naturally it fit into her hand, silky-smooth skin with ridged veins underneath. She moved her hand experimentally, and his deep groan made her look up at him. His eyes had drifted closed, but he opened them again to smile at her in reassurance.

"You've already got the right idea, angel. Try that again. Squeeze a little harder, you won't break it."

She stroked her hand down again, then up, rubbing her palm against the head, and his hips bucked upward. To her surprise, he grabbed her wrist to stop her. He grinned at her, but she could feel the tension all through him.

"I think," he said, "that's all I can take for now. If you really want to try everything."

Before she could protest, he enclosed her upper arms in his hands and guided her to straddle him, knees on either side of his hips, bodies pressed together from shoulder to hip with his cock trapped between them.

Her body had a will of its own, arching and rubbing

against him, feeling his skin and hair and muscle against her whole front as his arms wrapped around her back to hold her close. The sensation of being surrounded by his strength triggered a small twinge of the same panic that had frozen her body earlier, but he had been right. Sitting upright made her feel more free, more able to pull away if needed.

He grinned up at her. "You like this?"

"Yes," she said, and ducked her head to kiss him. His hands slid down to tilt her hips, and she gasped as his erection rubbed against her most sensitive flesh. It was delicious.

"I'll show you what to do," he murmured against her ear, "but you're in control. You can stop any time, and I swear I won't be angry."

"Word of a gentleman?"

"Yes. Word of a gentleman."

She swallowed hard, for courage, and then let him help her position herself over the broad head of his cock.

The head slipped inside first, and they both groaned, and then laughed. Experimentally, she wiggled a little lower, feeling her body expand to accommodate him. It carried a small sting, but it felt good, too, like stretching your legs over rough ground to reach the top of a hill.

She braced her hands on his shoulders as she lowered herself, inch by careful inch, until suddenly it seemed her inner muscles yielded all at once and she sank all the way down. The fullness was almost too much and she shivered for a long moment, wrapping her arms around his neck as he held her close, the support both soothing and arousing.

"Are you all right?" he murmured.

"I..." Experimentally, she moved upward, letting his shaft slide inside her, and they both groaned.

His hands slid back down to rest lightly on her hips. "Don't worry about me, angel. Do whatever feels good to you."

She began to move, slowly and then faster, shifting her hips until she found an angle that slid them together in a perfect rhythm, his hips arching upward as hers descended, going on and on until she whimpered in frustration.

He chuckled, though the sound was strained. "Here, angel, let me help you." And his hand went between their bodies to find the place where her pleasure gathered, stroking in time with her movements until fire rippled up her spine and she dissolved, her mouth finding his as she shuddered all around him, her knees clutching at his hips as she sagged against him.

With a groan, he pulled her off and took himself in hand. She watched in astonishment as he stroked himself, faster and harder, until he threw his head back with a final shout and a white liquid burst from the head of his cock.

He opened his eyes, and put an arm out to pull her closer as he kissed her. "Sorry."

"What was that?" She put out a careful finger to dab at the remnants of the liquid on his thigh, and he laughed.

"That, my curious angel, is what they call semen. If I had done that while I was still inside you, I could have left you with a baby."

"Oh," she said. "Mama explained that to me, but it's… different to actually see it."

He rolled from the bed and she slid further under the covers, yawning. She watched through half-lidded eyes as he washed himself and then brought a fresh cloth over to her, helping her wipe away the sweat and fluids. Then he blew out the candle and slid back into the bed, bringing her back against his front again, and she sighed in contentment as she fell asleep, more relaxed than she could ever remember being.

The next morning, Junia woke slowly, only to find Philip had already slipped from the bed and was dressing next to the fireplace. When she stirred, he looked over at her and smiled. "Good morning."

"Good morning," she said shyly. She burrowed into the covers, but never took her eyes off him. She would not have believed he could look even more handsome to her, but in this morning after their lovemaking, he rivaled the stars.

"I'm going to go talk to the innkeeper to see if there's a carriage we can rent. If there is, we could be back in London by this afternoon. I'll see if there's breakfast as well."

"Thank you."

He finished arranging his limp cravat as best he could and shrugged on his coat before crossing to the bed and bending down to kiss her. "You'd best get washed and dressed so we can leave as soon as we've eaten."

"All right."

He kissed her again as though he was already regretting leaving her, and then pulled away. She waited for him to lock the door behind himself before she leapt from the bed to wash and dress as quickly as she could. She tried to comb her hair, but had to give up doing any more of it than the top layers. She re-wrapped her hair with her scarf and tucked the edges in as best she could.

She crossed to the window and lifted a corner of the curtain to see there was a watery sun out, so the worst of the rain must be over. It would take them a good five or six hours to drive to London through the rutted and muddy roads, but they would be home again and ready to go rescue Pappa.

When Philip returned with the maid carrying a breakfast tray complete with a steaming coffee pot, Junia had prepared what few belongings they had so they could leave as soon as possible. Philip, too, seemed eager to leave, so they ate quickly.

"Were you able to get a carriage?"

He grimaced. "A gig. Pulled by a donkey. At least I will be returning you to your mother in style."

She giggled then sighed. He reached his hand across the table to cover hers, and she turned her hand to hold his.

"Don't worry, Junia. I'll bring him home safe."

She nodded, unwilling to trust her voice. Being able to share her worries with someone outside her family was a new sensation.

Philip left a sovereign on the tray for the housemaid, and they departed in the promised style in an ancient, creaking two-person gig behind a ragged donkey.

THE MORNING WAS CHILLY, so Philip insisted Junia wear his coat again. She only made a token protest, snuggling down into the body-warmed folds. As they drove, Junia heaved a sigh as a forgotten instruction finally came back to her.

"Pappa will scold me after we rescue him."

"And why is that?"

"Pappa always said if we had any trouble and he wasn't around to help, we should talk to Mr. Force about it. Pappa will say I should have sent Mr. Force a note instead of going off on my own." She had not even thought of it until this moment, now that she had someone else to talk to.

Philip frowned. "Mr. Force… wait a minute. Did your father want you to contact Taddeo Sforza?"

"Who?"

"Is Mr. Force a tall, mixed-race Italian man?"

Junia's jaw dropped. "Why, yes. Do you know him?"

He grinned at her. "Signore Sforza—Mr. Force—was my sister-in-law's man of business when she lived in Italy. He and his wife traveled here with Olivia four years ago, before she married my brother."

"That's an incredible coincidence."

"Not really. The community of blacks in London is fairly small, so the odds we would both know someone as prominent as Taddeo Sforza were high."

"Does he know your brother, the duke?"

"Of course. We'll pay Mr. Force a visit once we reassure your mother you're safe and have a chance to clean up."

Junia marveled to herself while he drove. When her family had escaped from America, she had never imagined they would meet anyone who knew a duke. Now she sat next to a duke's brother on their way to see another man who knew him.

❧

THE CLOSER THEY came to London, the more anxious Junia became, until she was all but vibrating next to him as they turned onto the street where her family lived.

Philip took one hand from the reins to cover hers. "Junia. It will be fine."

She smiled at him but didn't seem to relax much as she directed him to pull up in front of a small but tidy house on a quiet Islington street. A young man bustled up to hold the donkey's reins, and Philip tossed him one of his remaining coins before descending from the cart and handing Junia down from it.

As soon as her feet touched the ground, the front door of the house burst open and a young woman raced down the steps, shrieking with joy as she reached Junia. With a shock, Philip realized this must be Junia's younger sister Zillah. When he had last seen her, she had been a child of thirteen, scrawny and frightened. Now she was a young lady of seventeen who had clearly adapted to her new life, the same age Junia had been when the family escaped.

He stepped back to allow the sisters to have their reunion, and looked to the doorway where Junia's mother, Jerusha Reynolds, waited for her daughters. Even in a fashionably high-waisted dress, he could see she was heavily pregnant, which must have added to Junia's anxiety about rescuing her father as quickly as possible.

Rather than make the older woman descend the steps,

Philip walked to her, followed by Junia and Zillah, their arms still wrapped around each other. He bowed to her. "Mrs. Reynolds."

"Why, it's Major Avondale!" Her voice still carried the soft accents of Maryland, strange but warm on this English street. "Come in, come in. There's no need for all of us to make a spectacle of ourselves on the street."

Her daughters did not seem much abashed and each kissed their mother's cheek as they entered the house. Junia removed Philip's coat and handed it to him. Mrs. Reynolds gasped aloud.

"What on earth are you wearing, Junia?"

"I was a house servant, Mama, at the place where Pappa is being held prisoner." Philip noticed that, when speaking to her mother, Junia slipped back to her American accents. "It's a disguise."

"It's terrible," her mother said, and Zillah nodded in agreement, pulling a face. "We need to get you washed and dressed in your own clothes."

Mrs. Reynolds turned back to Philip. "I apologize I can't offer you hospitality at the moment, Major, but will you return tomorrow afternoon? I would like to thank you for bringing my daughter home safely."

"I would be honored, Mrs. Reynolds," Philip said. He shrugged into his coat and bowed over the hand she extended to him. "I need to check on my brother, in any case. Miss Junia will be able to tell you of our adventures." He spared a glance at her and felt a little pang at the thought of leaving. A full day and night in her company had felt like no time at all against the time they had spent apart. He was surprised at his reluctance to let her out of his sight again, even if only for a few hours.

He thought he saw a little of the same loss in her face when she took a step towards him. "But you can't just leave. What about my father?"

Before he could respond, her mother frowned at her. "What do you mean? Your Pappa came home last night."

❧　8　❧

Junia pulled away from Zillah, hiked up her skirts, and flew up the stairs, with Philip on her heels. She flung open the door to her parents' bedroom to see her father lying propped up against a multitude of pillows, frowning at a letter in his hand.

"Pappa!"

She ran to the bed and threw herself into his outstretched arms. He hugged her close, and she finally let the tears she had been suppressing for weeks flow as sobs of relief that he was safely home. Pappa rocked her as she cried, and she was certain she felt a few of his own tears on her forehead.

As she calmed, she straightened and looked around. Philip handed her a clean handkerchief from the table next to the bed, and she took a moment to wipe her eyes and blow her nose. He grinned at her, and she briefly stuck her tongue out at him from behind the cover of the handkerchief.

Her father's arm still around her, she leaned against his shoulder. "How did you get free?"

Caius Reynolds shook his head. "It was the strangest

thing. They came up to my room last night, loaded me into the cart, and brought me back. They barely stopped when they pushed me out in front of the house."

"Are you well? Why are you still in bed?"

"Your mother insisted." Her father rolled his eyes a bit, but was clearly pleased with this demonstration of wifely concern. "She did bring me the correspondence that stacked up while I was away, so I can get caught up on business."

Junia looked over at Philip, who was frowning in confusion. "Did they say anything about why they had taken you, or why they were returning you?"

"Not a thing."

"That's enough now, Junia," her mother said from the doorway. "Let your father rest." Junia sighed and stood up from the bed, Philip's hand under her elbow briefly steadying her until she got her footing.

Mama came into the room and fussed with her husband's pillows until he seized her hand and kissed it. She bent to kiss him and then rest her forehead against his for a long moment.

Zillah watched from the doorway with a little smirk, and Junia scowled at her.

"I need to see what my brother has been doing, and get some fresh clothes," Philip said. "I will see you tomorrow, J… Miss Junia."

He bowed over her hand, bowed to her parents, and even bowed to the giggling Zillah before leaving the room.

Junia frowned after him for a long moment, feeling a strange panic as he disappeared from her sight. The small time they had carved out to be together had ended before she was ready, and the abrupt return to reality made her stomach lurch unpleasantly.

Zillah grasped her by the elbow and steered Junia out of the room towards the one they shared.

"We'll get you a bath, and wash your hair, and see if those mats will come out," Zillah said. "And then you're going to tell me *everything*."

Junia laughed, because she knew she was never going to tell her baby sister *everything*.

LACKING the key he had dropped when he had been abducted, Philip knocked at the door of the flat he shared with Peter. Their manservant opened the door and his jaw dropped. "Major Avondale!"

"Hello, Nelson. Is Peter here?"

"He returned home yesterday. He was quite upset to hear you had disappeared."

"I'm sure he was."

As Philip walked down the short hallway towards their drawing room, the door was jerked open and Peter stood in the entrance, scowling at him.

"Where in the *hell* have you been?" Peter said. "I've been worried sick!"

"Isn't a curate supposed to watch his language and set an example for his flock?" Philip grinned at his brother as he passed him and continued on into the drawing room. He sank into one of the armchairs in front of the fire with a sigh of relief. Now that he was finally home, he was almost too tired to move.

"They're mostly sailors. They think I don't swear nearly enough." Peter closed the door and followed Philip, standing behind the chair set on the other side. He frowned at his brother as Philip sprawled more comfortably, propping his boots on the edge of the grate. "What happened?"

"I was abducted by villains."

"You're joking."

"Not in the least." Philip tilted his head up to look Peter in the eye. "I was abducted because they thought I was you."

Peter's jaw dropped. "I don't believe it!"

"Neither did I," Philip said dryly, "but the fact they kept calling me 'parson' made me realize they'd got the wrong man."

Peter fell heavily into his chair. "I was only trying to help."

Philip groaned. "That's always where you go wrong. Stop helping people!"

"I have to. I'm a minister." Peter looked pious, and Philip sighed. It was demmed awkward having an idealist as your twin brother.

Peter sighed as well and scrubbed his hands through his hair, tousling his already disarrayed curls even more. "As I said, most of my parishioners are sailors. One of them came to me after morning services, hat in hand, and he asked me what the Lord thought of smuggling."

"And what did you say?"

"I admitted that the Lord frowned upon it. And the man said it was even worse, because they were bringing the contraband through the graveyard at St. Luke's."

Philip sat up abruptly. "The devil you say!"

"You may be sure I investigated and searched all around,

but I could find no evidence it was happening. Still, men did seem to be lurking about at strange hours, so it seemed there must be something to it. And then my informant disappeared."

A sudden dread hit Philip. "He wasn't a black man, was he? A middle-aged man in his forties or so?"

"No, no, nothing like," Peter said, and Philip huffed a small sigh of relief. "He was a young man, and an Englishman. Sandy hair, plenty of freckles. Kentish, so I went there to look for him."

"If he got involved with Kentish smugglers, he's likely dead at the bottom of the Channel by now. They don't appreciate any competition."

"That's what I feared, but I had to look for him anyway. I had no luck at all, so I came back to London after a few days, only to find *you* mysteriously disappeared as well."

"There must have been something to it, assuming the men who kidnapped me were part of the same gang," Philip said. "But it seems as though that lead came to a dead end."

"But where have you *been*? I was getting ready to send a message to Paul if you hadn't turned up by today."

Philip snorted. "What did you think Paul was going to be able to do?" Their elder brother might be a duke, but he was certainly not acquainted with the criminal class.

"I don't know. Hire a Bow Street runner, most likely. You know I haven't the funds for one."

Philip shook his head. "Are you acquainted with a man named Caius Reynolds? He's as I described him earlier—a middle-aged black man, originally from America. About medium height, balding, with some weight around the middle."

Peter shook his head in turn. "I've never heard of him, and the description is not familiar."

"Damn." Philip rubbed his face, feeling the scratchiness of the extra growth of beard that had overtaken his carefully groomed sidewhiskers. "I need a bath. And some sleep. And then we can puzzle it out some more."

"You're not going to tell me where you've been?"

"I hardly know myself. Northwest of London. Near a forest. The route we took back was so circuitous that I'm not sure I could say where the house was that we were held."

"'We'? Who did you travel with?"

Philip flushed. "None of your business."

"Oh ho! Like that, is it?"

"Not at all," Philip said stiffly. "She is a respectable lady who required my assistance."

"I look forward to hearing all about her over supper." Peter grinned, and Philip wanted to plant him a facer.

He now had Peter's information, but very little knowledge from it. The situation became more confusing by the moment.

He would discuss it with Junia tomorrow, and perhaps try to get more details from her father. The mere thought of seeing her again gave him a warm glow he did not want to examine while his twin's mocking eye was on him.

AFTER SUPPER AND A LONG, luxurious bath, Junia sat between Zillah's feet as her sister patiently wielded a wide-toothed comb to coax the mats out of Junia's curly hair. Their mother sat in an armchair in the corner of their room, clearly reluctant to allow her older daughter out of her sight again.

Junia smiled at her. "You see, Mama? It all came right in the end."

Her mother frowned. "It was thanks to the Lord you returned home safely."

"And Major Avondale," Zillah said cheerfully. Mama glared at her before returning her attention to Junia, clearly on the verge of asking a question Junia did not want to answer. Thankfully, Zillah rescued her with a sharp tug of the comb.

"Ouch!"

"Sorry, sorry," Zillah said, and Junia bit back her smile.

When her hair was combed and wrapped for the night, their mother said, "Zillah."

"Yes, Mama?"

"Go down to the kitchen and ask Mrs. Higgins to make your sister a cotton bark posset."

"Can't Sally do it?"

"Sally's been run off her feet all day helping us. Besides, I want you to do it."

Zillah looked from one to the other of them before sighing deeply and getting to her feet. "Yes, Mama."

Mama waited for the door to close before patting her lap. "Come here, honey."

With a sigh, Junia scooted over and lay her head in her mother's lap like she had done since she was a small girl, her mother gently stroking her shoulders and back to soothe her. The circumstances were different—better—but the comfort was the same even though Junia was grown now.

"Junia?"

"Yes, Mama?"

Her mother hesitated for a long moment, and then said, "You know that man can't ever marry you, don't you?"

"I know he can't, Mama." There were too many differences between them, and those had become increasingly clear the longer she lived in London. Even the richest merchant's daughter could barely dream of marrying a duke's brother, and that was even before Junia considered her race, and her nationality, and the fact most Englishmen expected to marry a virgin, and the smallness of the dowry her father could provide compared to what a duke's brother would expect. She was, in every way, the opposite of what his family would want when it came to choosing his bride.

"I'm sorry, honey."

Junia lifted her hand, and her mother took it in a strong, comforting grip. "Just let me dream a little longer. Please?"

"All right."

They sat together by the fire, Junia taking comfort in her mother's steadfast love, until Zillah returned with the posset. After only a moment's hesitation, Junia drank it down.

Taking the precaution was for the best. For both of them.

❧   9   ❧

The next day, Junia regarded herself in the mirror with satisfaction, finally feeling confident in her appearance again. The bright jonquil yellow of her stylish muslin gown made her skin glow as if illuminated from within. Zillah helped arrange her curls into fashionable puffs and topped them with a frivolous little lace cap adorned with coordinating ribbons. Her hands were still a little rough from her masquerade, but a good dose of her mother's hand cream and wearing cotton gloves overnight had smoothed them fairly well.

Finally, Philip would see her wearing something other than ill-fitting hand-me-downs or threadbare, dirty servant's clothing.

He's seen you in much less, a sly voice inside her said, and she cast her eyes down to hide the little smile of remembrance.

"What is it?" Zillah asked.

"Nothing," Junia said, and slid a set of thin gold bangles onto her wrist. "Are you ready to go downstairs?"

~

"Who are you?" a tiny voice piped from somewhere behind him.

Philip turned, hat still in hand, to see a small boy who appeared to be about two years old standing in the hallway. He was dressed in a rumpled blue playsuit, staring up at Philip curiously. His curly hair was twisted into small knots all over his head, presumably to keep it neat and tidy.

Philip got down on one knee. "I am Major Avondale. And who might you be?"

"I'm George. Nya come home last night."

"That she did," Philip said, deducing that "Nya" must be Junia. "And your Pappa as well?"

George nodded. His thumb rose to his mouth as he continued to stare at Philip.

"George Caius Reynolds, what are you—oh!"

Philip rose swiftly to his feet and bowed to Junia's mother. "Good afternoon, Mrs. Reynolds."

She clucked her tongue. "Did that girl wander off before she could come tell me you were here? I don't know what I'm going to do with her. It's hard enough to find servants in the city as it is." Mrs. Reynolds stopped, took a breath to gather herself, and smiled warmly at him, a small glint of irony in her eye. "Please, come in and sit down."

She took George by the hand to lead him up the stairs and through the open door of the drawing room, with Philip following close behind. The same servant who had answered the door and then gone upstairs appeared in the doorway, breathless and cap askew.

"Master George! I've been looking everywhere for you.

I'm that sorry, Mrs. Reynolds—he got away from Kitty when she was trying to get him fed and she asked me to help her look."

"Never mind now, Sally," Mrs. Reynolds said. "Please take George back to the nursery and then bring up the tea tray."

"Yes, ma'am," Sally said, taking George by the hand and leading him towards the stairs to the second floor. She scolded him under her breath as they walked, but George looked back at Philip instead, who winked at him. George ducked his head bashfully as the pair disappeared from view.

Philip helped Mrs. Reynolds into a chair by the unlit fireplace and seated himself on the small settee nearby. The furniture was clearly not new—it had likely come with the house when they purchased it—but it was well-polished and had been re-covered in fresh, bright fabrics that made the room a cozy space to gather.

He rose as Junia and Zillah entered the room arm-in-arm, glowing and confident. Junia was the very picture of a fashionable young lady about town, and she took his breath away. He barely recognized her as his Junia, but admired her even more. Her ability to adapt to a new country and her new status as a free, middle-class young woman demonstrated an inner strength even beyond what he had seen in her when they first met.

She extended her free hand to him and he bowed over it, his lips brushing against her knuckles in a kiss that was only perceptible to the two of them. He could feel her repressed shiver as she smiled at him and squeezed his hand in return, sending only the smallest of glances towards her mother.

"Good afternoon, Miss Reynolds," Philip said. "I'm glad

to see you seem to be no worse for the wear after your adventure."

Her mother cleared her throat, and Junia dropped his hand as though she had been burned. Philip turned to Zillah and bowed to her as well. "Miss Zillah, so lovely to see you again."

Like any seventeen-year-old in adult company, Zillah giggled and ducked her head. "Thank you, Major."

He settled Junia onto the settee with Zillah next to her and took one of the chairs across from the three women. A flashing look from Junia told him she, too, regretted they could not sit together under her mother's stern eye. Sally returned with the tea tray, her cap and dignity back in place, and set it on the small table in front of Junia.

"Shall I pour, Mama?" Junia asked, and her mother nodded.

Philip accepted his cup with a smile and said, "Will Mr. Reynolds be joining us?"

"Not today," Mrs. Reynolds said. "I want him to rest one day longer before he goes back to his office."

Philip cleared his throat. "I'm embarrassed to realize I did not ask what business Mr. Reynolds has established himself in."

"We own a counting-house," Zillah said proudly, and Philip nodded, impressed. Given Caius Reynolds' facility with numbers, it was a natural choice.

"We used to live above it," Junia put in, "but Pappa has been successful enough to buy this house."

"Enough, girls." Mrs. Reynolds looked embarrassed but a little pleased. "Major Avondale doesn't need to know every detail."

"But I *am* interested, ma'am," he said. "I'm pleased to see how well your family has prospered since I last saw you four years ago."

"Thank you, Major. Are you on leave from the army?"

Philip took another sip from the cup in his hand. "No, I sold out a few months ago. One of my mother's aunts left me a small property in Gloucestershire in her will, and I was tired of army life."

"I'm glad you made it safely through the wars, Major," Junia said, her voice warm.

He looked at her and smiled. "So am I." She ducked her head shyly, and his smile grew broader. He would be content to sit here with her for the rest of the afternoon, if he could.

Philip pulled his gaze away from her as multiple footsteps sounded up the stairs and the drawing room door opened.

"My dear Miss Reynolds! How glad I am to see you recovered from your illness."

As he rose to his feet, Philip examined the two young men who stood in the doorway of the Reynolds's drawing room. They could not have made a stronger contrast to one another if they had planned for a week. One was tall and cadaverously thin, with white-blond hair and pale blue eyes to match, dressed in clothes that hung off him like a scarecrow.

The other was short and a little rotund even at his young age, with hair and eyes as dark as his friend's were light. Philip judged him to be not older than three-and-twenty, but he dressed like a much older man in clothes that were at least ten years out of fashion. He carried a nosegay of violets in one hand and presented them to Junia with a flourish as he bowed low to her.

Philip was surprised by his little flare of jealousy. Was this a suitor of Junia's? It had not occurred to him before, but of course she must have suitors in her new position as a respectable merchant's daughter. He tried to keep a scowl off his face at the thought.

The tall man made his bow as well, first to Junia and Zillah, and then to their mother before glancing around the room. When his gaze landed on Philip, he saw the younger man's eyes widen in surprise before quickly concealing his reaction.

Interesting. Very *interesting.*

The rotund man finished his speech to Junia and watched in satisfaction as she gave a token sniff to his floral offering before setting it aside with a smile. He, too, looked around the room, and made a quickly concealed start when he saw Philip. Philip was almost certain he, too, recognized him, but Philip was equally certain he had never seen either of them before in his life.

The rotund man said, "I see your parents have made a new friend, Miss Reynolds. Will you introduce us?"

"Of course. Major Lord Philip Avondale, this is Mr. Williams and Mr. Hughes."

Mr. Williams was the pale, tall one; Mr. Hughes, the darker and shorter. The three men bowed to each other, Philip deliberately keeping his expression neutral and pleasant.

"How do you know the family, Major?" Williams said.

"I met them on their voyage from America, four years ago. When I came to London, I decided to look them up and pay my respects."

"So you have only recently returned to London?" Williams asked.

"Yes," Philip said, with perfect, if incomplete, truth.

"I feel perhaps we have met before, Major Avondale," Hughes said, confirming Philip's suspicion he was the bolder of the two.

Philip kept his expression bland. "I do not believe so, Mr. Hughes. Your face is not at all familiar to me."

"Hm. I don't suppose you have a twin," Hughes said, and laughed heartily. Philip only smiled, and glanced over at Junia. She looked a little puzzled, but was clearly willing to follow his lead and not reveal any information.

Mrs. Reynolds said, "Won't you sit down, gentlemen?"

Williams and Hughes each took a chair across from the ladies, while Philip propped his shoulder against the fireplace mantel in a spot that allowed him to watch everyone. Junia was cordial, but did not seem to show any particular favor to either man as they exchanged commonplaces about the weather and the dreadful price of necessities. Sally bustled in with more teacups and hot water, and bustled out again.

"And how is Mr. Reynolds?" Hughes asked at last. "Was he felled by the same malady as Miss Reynolds?"

"I'm afraid so," Mrs. Reynolds said. "But he is recovering now and should be back in the office in another day or two." Philip took note of this prevarication—clearly, the Reynolds family did not want outsiders to know about the abduction, or that Junia had gone in pursuit of the kidnappers.

Junia looked over at Philip, a smile crossing her face. "I forgot to mention Mr. Hughes and Mr. Williams work in my father's counting-house, as junior clerks."

"I am a full clerk now, Miss Reynolds," Hughes said in what he undoubtedly meant to be a jesting tone, but came out with an edge of irritation. "Surely your father mentioned that to you."

"I'm afraid I haven't much of a head for business," Junia said sadly. "So much of what Pappa says goes in one ear and out the other."

Philip coughed to hide his chuckle. To his eyes, Junia was not very convincing as a feather-witted young woman, but Hughes relaxed a little and smiled a condescending little smile at her. "Of course not. Ladies have so many other things to think about."

When an interminable twenty minutes had passed and a cup of tea had been drunk by each of them, Hughes looked at his friend and both men rose to their feet. "I suppose we ought to be going, Mrs. Reynolds," Hughes said. "We only wanted to call to see how Mr. Reynolds was getting on."

Hughes looked over at Philip, who smiled and remained planted in his spot. Philip knew the other man was trying to think of a discreet way to ask why Philip showed no sign of leaving when it was well past the polite length of time for an afternoon call.

"Miss Reynolds has agreed to stroll in the park with me," Philip said. The falsehood rolled smoothly off his tongue. "She was just about to fetch her bonnet when you gentlemen called."

Junia immediately rose to her feet and smiled at each man in turn. "I certainly was. If you will excuse me?"

Hughes and Williams had no choice but to bow to each of the women, and then to Philip, and take their leave. Philip strained to listen for any muttered conversation as they left, but heard nothing. That seemed perhaps more ominous than if they had talked.

"I'll get my bonnet now," Junia said, and he smiled and bowed to her from his spot at the fireplace.

Junia's mother regarded him thoughtfully. "Zillah, why don't you go help Junia get ready?"

Zillah pouted, but got to her feet. "I always have to miss the *interesting* conversations." With a toss of her head, she followed Junia from the room, closing the door firmly behind herself.

"Please, sit down, Major."

Philip could feel himself flush and hoped it wasn't too noticeable. If he wasn't mistaken, he was about to be asked his intentions by Junia's mother, and he wasn't certain what his answer would be. Not yet, anyway.

"We do appreciate your help, Major Avondale, very much," Mrs. Reynolds said, "but it's best you don't call on us again after today."

Philip blinked. "I see." She certainly saw no value in mincing her words.

"We both know there's nothing that can come of your friendship with Junia. She's a respectable young woman who can expect to marry well within our little society here, where the gentlemen understand what we came from and make allowances, unlike in your world. She doesn't have to settle as an aristocrat's mistress."

Philip winced. "I appreciate your plain speaking, Mrs. Reynolds."

The older woman sighed. "I wish the world was different. I like you very much, I always have. I think you and Junia would do well together. But we both know your family would never allow it."

"I'm nearly thirty, Mrs. Reynolds." He knew his voice was

stiff to conceal the stab of rejection. "I don't allow my family to dictate who I can marry."

She smiled sadly at him. "It's not just your family. It's the whole world. I don't want to see my Junia get hurt."

"I understand."

He knew she spoke the truth about the practical realities of her family's situation. That didn't help the ache in his chest at the thought of having to let Junia go a second time, not now when he....

The door opened, and Junia floated in with a cerulean blue spencer over her yellow gown and a frivolous wide-brimmed bonnet perched on her head. She was a little breathless and still pulling on her short gloves as she looked from one to the other of them.

"Is anything wrong?" Junia said.

"Nothing, honey," Mrs. Reynolds said. "Go have your walk now."

Frowning, Junia bent and kissed her mother's proffered cheek before turning to Philip. "Shall we go, Major?"

Philip bowed low, knowing he had met a worthy opponent this day. "Good afternoon, Mrs. Reynolds."

"Goodbye, Major."

10

A s they walked out the front door, Philip led Junia down the stairs and then tucked her hand into the crook of his arm as they walked. She suppressed a little sigh of happiness at being alone with him once more.

"Where shall we go first?" she asked.

"Towards St. Luke's. We can see if anything looks peculiar or different from when you last saw it."

"We don't attend that church very often," she said, a little apologetically. "We usually go to the dissenting church. But George was baptized at St. Luke's since Pappa said it's best to be church members if you want to enter a profession later on."

"That's likely why you haven't met Peter," Philip said. "He only became a curate there about a year ago."

"I don't entirely understand the system, but you and your brother are lords, the younger sons of a duke. Shouldn't he have a… a… "

"A better posting? More elegant, or more lucrative?"

"Well, yes."

"It's what he prefers. He would rather serve in a parish where he feels he can do some good than the prosperous sort our brother holds the livings of." Philip sighed. "But sometimes Peter is a little *too* eager to do good. I can't tell you how many times I've had to pull him out of scrapes thanks to his idealism, and it looks like this is yet another one where he got in over his head because he wanted to help someone."

Junia laughed. "Zillah is an idealist, too. I can't tell you how many mangy dogs she's tried to rescue or beggars she's emptied her purse for. We must make sure they never meet."

"Yes," Philip said, and something dimmed in him.

Junia looked at him curiously. "Is anything wrong?"

He shook himself a little and smiled down at her so warmly that her heart gave a little leap. "No, no. Everything's fine. Tell me more about Zillah. I've always wondered how she had adapted to living in England."

Junia began relating a few light, amusing stories about her sister, but Philip's mood had definitely shifted.

She wondered again what he and her mother had been talking about to make them both look so grim when she had entered the drawing room earlier.

St. Luke's had been built less than a hundred years before, which seemed quite old to Junia until she thought about the many even older buildings that surrounded them in London. There was nothing very remarkable about it, but Philip frowned thoughtfully as they wandered through the grounds and into the graveyard.

"How far is it from here to your father's counting-house?"

Junia looked around with a frown. "Not far. Two streets over. Do you think that has something to do with it?"

"I don't know. But it seems significant." He sighed. "I think I would need Peter to come with me to look inside the church itself since it's usually locked during the day. Let's walk over to the counting-house."

As they walked, Philip said, "Where did your father get the money to start his counting-house? Such a venture usually requires a fairly large amount of capital to start."

Junia tossed her head, but looked away, bracing herself for his reaction. "He had been saving money to buy our freedom, but most of it came from Mr. Reynolds. Our old master. It was our back wages for the four of us, Pappa said. He even left a receipt for the exact amount, minus room and board."

Philip paused and looked down at her for a long moment. Then a smile crept across his face, and she couldn't help but smile back, relief washing through her. "How very clever," he said, and they began walking again.

As they drew closer to her father's counting-house, Philip's steps slowed almost to a stop. Junia looked up to see his face had become distant and abstracted.

"Philip? Is something wrong?"

A passerby bumped into Philip from the opposite direction and, after instinctively checking his pockets, he began walking again.

"What if," he said slowly, "what if the reason the work they had your father doing seemed nonsensical because it *was* nonsensical? What if they were holding him prisoner because they needed him to be away from the counting-house, or from another place where he does business?"

She shook her head. "But that makes no more sense."

"It does, though. You have no brother to check up on the business. Your mother could not have been there to oversee it, not in her condition. You and Zillah don't know how to run the business, and you were away yourself."

Junia gasped as she understood what he was saying. "You think maybe they kidnapped Pappa to keep him away from whatever it was they were trying to do, not because they wanted *him* to do something."

"Exactly." Philip frowned. "We need ask your father what properties he controls or owns other than your house and the counting-house. It could be a warehouse or similar building that's being used for nefarious purposes. Let's look at the counting-house first."

PHILIP LOOKED around as they walked, his instincts telling him someone was watching them, though he could not see anyone. He pulled Junia a little closer and she smiled up at him. He couldn't help smiling back.

He knew he was being foolish. She had been too young for them to be more than acquaintances while aboard ship, though he had admired her courage and resilience even then. Now, with barely a week's re-acquaintance, he admired her even more. It had taken strength of will and character for her to decide to rescue her father, even at great risk to herself. He admired her whole family, in fact. It was not easy to flee to a strange country and not only survive, but thrive. The desperate refugees he had met four years ago were now a prosperous middle-class merchant family. Philip had no illusions that it had been easy for them.

And as the younger brother of a duke, he was as out of reach for their daughter as one of the stars in the sky as far as her family was concerned.

He could at least do her this service of finding out why her father had been kidnapped and held prisoner, even if it would be the only service he could provide before he respected her mother's wishes and walked away.

"Here it is," Junia said.

The words shook him out of his gloom as they stopped in front of a medium-sized building with small, high windows on either side of a solid front door. A counting-house needed to be a secure place so clients would be comfortable having their money and accounts kept there. There was a second row of larger windows above that Junia pointed to.

"That's the flat where we lived until Pappa bought the house a year ago."

"Is it empty now?"

Junia frowned. "I would need to ask. I can't remember if my parents decided to rent it out or leave it vacant to make the building more secure."

Philip examined the windows thoughtfully. The curtains were drawn, and the rooms beyond seemed to be dark. If anyone lived there, he could see no sign.

Philip opened the door of the office for Junia and followed her into the main room. Rows of clerks sat at rows of desks, heads bent over their account books as they scribbled away. He looked around to see if he could spot Hughes or Williams, but neither man seemed to be in the room.

Instead, a young lad of about fifteen approached them. Like many of the other apprentices in the room, he was clearly of African descent. Junia's father seemed to have a policy of hiring apprentices with a similar background to his own. Philip applauded the gesture—he knew it was often difficult to get an apprenticeship without a family connection, even among the middle classes.

Junia smiled as the apprentice bowed to her. "Good afternoon, Michael."

"Good afternoon, miss."

"Major Avondale, this is Michael Smith."

After they exchanged bows, Philip said, "Are Mr. Hughes and Mr. Williams here?"

"No, sir. They took the afternoon off." Michael frowned, as if disapproving of this sloth on a working day.

"I see," Philip said. "As we were walking up, Miss Reynolds and I wondered if there is a tenant in the upstairs apartment."

Michael shook his head. "It's not rented out. I wouldn't stay there if you gave me a million pounds. There's a ghost lives up there."

Philip and Junia exchanged looks, and Philip said, "Really? How do you know?"

"We can hear it walking at night, but when anyone goes up to look, there's no one there."

"No one there?"

Michael shook his head. "Just the furniture all covered up with sheets."

Junia started, and Philip put a calming hand on her arm. "Thank you, Michael."

The boy nodded and threaded his way through the desks back to his own.

Philip drew back towards the entrance, gently guiding Junia with a hand at her elbow.

"Something about what he said surprised you. What was it?"

"There shouldn't be any furniture up there," Junia said quietly. "We brought everything to the townhouse with us when we moved."

11

As they walked back to the townhouse, Junia could not help but be affected by Philip's suppressed gloom. The realization that her family might still be in danger from unknown persons made her own stomach tighten with nausea.

"It must be one of your father's employees," Philip said. "Or a business associate. Someone close to all of you."

Junia shivered. "That almost makes it worse. I worried less when I thought he had been taken by total strangers. But for it to have been someone we know…"

"Traitors always leave chaos in their wake." Philip's voice was grim, perhaps remembering his years at war. "The breach of trust is almost worse than any action they might take."

"What are we going to do?"

"*We* are not going to do anything," Philip said. "*I* will go back tonight after it gets dark and see if there's any activity at the building."

"You can't go alone. It will be dangerous."

"I'll take Peter with me. Or your father. Probably both of them." He fixed her with a stern glare. "But *you*, angel, will wait at home. I can't be worrying about you while I'm trying to investigate what's going on."

Junia frowned, but before she could argue, they arrived in front of her family's house. Philip took her by the shoulders and turned her to him. "Promise me, Junia."

She looked up at him, a little breathless at the intensity of his expression, and she saw his eyes darken as his gaze focused on her lips. Without conscious thought, she swayed toward him, wanting him to kiss her, not caring they were on a public street in view of anyone passing by.

A sharp rap on the front window carried to them and Philip stepped back, his hands dropping away but his eyes still intense on her. "Promise me."

The rap came again, and Junia turned to speed up the stairs to the front door. You didn't wait when Mama knocked twice. Sally opened it promptly and glared at Philip before announcing to the whole street, "Your mama wants to see you in the drawing room, Miss Reynolds."

Junia gave a helpless little wave to Philip, still standing on the walkway, and began unbuttoning her pelisse to hand to Sally, a little burst of relief bubbling inside her.

She might be in for a scolding from Mama, but the interruption had prevented her from making Philip a promise she had no intention of keeping.

To Philip's surprise, Peter balked at the idea of breaking into someone else's property to look for smugglers.

"I'm a curate now," Peter said. "I can't go around breaking into flats and catching criminals. Besides, Paul said if I got into one more scrape, he would give me that living in Yorkshire, and I would have to take it. I would hate living in Yorkshire."

Under normal circumstances, Philip would have been all in favor of Peter moving to Yorkshire to keep him out of mischief, but of course the one time he needed his twin to act like his usual reckless self was the time Peter had decided to try to do better.

"You can't leave me to do this alone. It's your fault I'm involved in this in the first place."

"I didn't do it on purpose."

"That's always your excuse."

Peter narrowed his eyes. "I can't believe you're the one who wants to do this. I thought you hated lost causes."

"It's not a lost cause. I think we can win."

"And what will you win?" Peter said with unexpected shrewdness, and Philip felt himself flush.

"Oh ho!" Peter crowed. "Like that, is it?"

"Like what?"

"Like you playing knight in shining armor to a damsel in distress."

Philip remembered Junia's absolute determination to free her father and her uncomplaining trek with him to safety when he knew she must have been exhausted and frightened. "There is a damsel, but she's stronger than you give her credit for."

Peter eyed him shrewdly. "Are you planning to marry the chit?"

Philip was silent for a long moment. If he thought about

it rationally, he knew it was impossible. Her family would oppose it. His mother would dissolve into hysterics. All of high society would be shocked and appalled that Lord Philip Avondale, the son and brother of the Duke of Livesey, had married a woman who was not only of another race, but a former slave, and an American, *and* a merchant's daughter, to boot.

But in his heart, he couldn't bring himself to care what anyone's opinions were, as long as Junia would have him. If she agreed to marry him, he would let the rest of the world burn.

"Yes," Philip said. "It's like that."

"Well, then," Peter said. "I suppose we had better form our plan. If you're hoping to woo a wife into the bargain, we'll need to make sure you don't break your neck."

Junia listened to her mother's scolding with half an ear, frowning, smiling, and agreeing in the right places even as she allowed herself to dream about Philip instead, and worry about his plans for that night. After several minutes, her mother sighed.

"I suppose I can't tell you anything about being careful with your feelings, even if it is for your own good."

"Oh, Mama." Junia stood up and crossed to her mother's chair to kiss her cheek. "I do listen to you."

"You're a woman grown now, and most of the other girls your age around here are already married," Mama said. "Your Pappa and I, we just want you to be settled and happy."

"How is Pappa today? I wanted to go up and see him, but I don't want to bother him."

Her mother relaxed a little. "He's much better. Go up and see him. Maybe *he* can talk some sense into you."

Junia laughed and ran up the stairs, feeling more lighthearted than she had in ages. Perhaps ever.

In her parents' room, she found her father sitting at his desk, fully dressed and with his spectacles on as he read through some correspondence. He smiled at her as she came in, and she eyed him critically. The bruises on his face were fading, and the scrapes were nearly healed.

"How are you, Pappa?"

"Much better, honey, much better. All I really needed was some food and rest."

Junia crossed to sit in a chair near her father's. "Major Avondale and I have been investigating to try and find out who did this to you."

Her father frowned. "You shouldn't be doing that. It could be dangerous."

"We're worried there may be some action happening in the next few days. Perhaps tonight. And that the criminals could be someone we already know."

Junia spelled out all of their information and guesses to her father, from the reason why he had been kidnapped to the possible traitors in their midst. He listened thoughtfully, asking a few pointed questions but mostly allowing Junia to speak.

"If you had to guess, who do you think might have done this?"

Pappa leaned back in his chair, lost in thought. "At the bottom, it's not very clever. A lot has counted on being able to hold onto people who were able to get away. He's likely right that it's smugglers."

"Phi—Major Avondale thinks it could be one of your clerks, or a business associate."

Pappa's brows raised at her slip, but he must have decided to let it pass, because when he spoke, he only said, "It could be. I think he's right—I think it's someone we know."

"Mr. Hughes and Mr. Williams called this afternoon."

"Your mama told me. What did they have to say?"

"Not much." Junia frowned. "They barely even asked about you. He didn't say it, but I think that's who Major Avondale suspects."

"Whom do you suspect?"

"It could be them. I never thought they were very bright."

"Considering how the scheme has gone so far, that might not be a point against their guilt." He frowned and rubbed his forehead. "Let me think and see if there's anyone else who might make sense."

Junia felt instantly remorseful—her father was still recovering, and here she was pressing him to answer questions. "Of course, Pappa. I only brought it up since Major Avondale will be investigating tonight."

"You care for him, don't you?" Pappa said, and Junia gaped at him. She had hoped her feelings were not so obvious, but clearly her father had seen right through her.

"I… don't worry, Pappa. Mama already talked to me. I know he can never… we can't ever…"

As her voice trailed off, her father reached out to take her hand. "It depends on what a man really wants," he said unexpectedly. "If he's found the right woman, a man will move heaven and earth to keep her. Your mama and I were kept apart, threatened with separation, didn't see each other for months at a time even after we were wed. But I knew she was the right woman for me, so I did everything I could to stick by her."

"Even escaping and coming to a whole new country."

"No, Junia." He squeezed her hand. "We did that for you and your sister. And now George and the new baby, who don't have to grow up the way you did, or the way your mama and I did. Life will still be hard, but they'll be free in a way we never were. I want you to use every bit of freedom you have."

Junia stood up from her chair and leaned down to embrace him. His arms closed strong around her as she clung to him like the child she no longer was. When she finally straightened, he smiled at her.

"I don't know if it'll work out. None of us do. But it might be worth giving him a chance."

As he and Peter prepared to leave, there was a soft knock on the door of their flat. Nelson opened it to reveal a young man who seemed familiar. After a moment, Philip realized it was the one who had held the mule outside Junia's house.

"Package for Major Reynolds," the boy said, and held his hand out for a tip. Philip dropped a shilling on his palm, and the boy's fingers closed over it greedily before he darted away as though fearing Philip would change his mind.

He opened the package to find a key inside, but no note or writing on the envelope. He frowned at it, puzzled.

"What do you suppose it's a key for?" Peter asked.

"It's got to be the key to the flat. But why would Junia send it over without a note?"

"Women," Peter said, and turned away to shrug on his overcoat. Philip continued to frown at the key. There was something wrong here.

With a sigh, Philip put the key in his pocket. There now

seemed to be a good chance they were about to walk into a trap, but if the alternative was letting the kidnappers get away with their crimes, Philip was willing to stick his hand out and see what happened. He was strung taut because of the unknown ahead, but knew the confrontation was inevitable.

"Are you ready?" Philip asked.

"As ready as I can be," Peter said. "You're not really going to use that pistol, are you?"

"Only if I have to. I hope I won't."

"Lord preserve us if the bishop finds out." His face drawn into lines of gloom, Peter followed Philip down to the street, where they hailed a hackney coach and climbed in. The ride was tense, and Peter seemed disinclined to conversation.

"You're not letting a little danger worry you, are you?" Philip said with a smirk.

Peter glared at him through the darkness. "When you get in this knight-errant mood, I worry. But I know there's no dissuading you at this point. We're more alike than you prefer to admit."

When they were within a few blocks of the Reynolds house, Philip rapped on the roof of the carriage to have the driver let them out and paid the man off. Peter frowned as he saw the residential street.

"I thought we were going to the counting-house."

"We need to talk to Caius Reynolds first. I don't trust this mystery key that appeared so conveniently. But since the house is likely being watched, we'd better go in through the mews."

"At least I didn't wear my new boots," Peter grumbled,

but he followed along through the alley behind the homes until they stood at the back door of the Reynolds house. A light burned inside and Philip could hear a chatter of voices, so he rapped at the door.

A dark-skinned woman, her hair wrapped in an intricate headcloth, opened the door and glared at them. "What do you want, then?"

"We must see Mr. Reynolds at once," Philip said. He felt the way he always had before a battle, a mix of elation and dread, this time with an added edge of anxiety for the safety of Junia and her family. "Kindly take us to him."

She peered uncertainly from one to the other of them, clearly taken aback both by Philip's aristocratic accent and the fact they were twins. Peter smiled at her reassuringly, and she shook her head. She stepped back from the door to gesture them in.

"I'll have Sally take you up, I suppose."

Philip nodded and stepped into the neatly kept kitchen. In the corner, a young scullery maid goggled at the fine gentlemen entering their house through the back.

"Go fetch Sally, that's a good girl," the housekeeper said, and the scullery maid darted away. The housekeeper went back to her work as Philip and Peter waited a respectful distance away.

In his study, Reynolds looked from one to the other of them. "You think they're using the flat above my offices to hide their smuggled goods?"

"Yes, sir."

The older man removed his spectacles and rubbed his forehead. "Junia said you thought the culprits might be some of my own employees."

"It would make the most sense. It would explain why they needed you out of the way, and gave you work to keep you occupied. Those may have been books kept by the smugglers to keep track of their activities that needed to be altered for some reason, and they took advantage of having you at hand."

"What's your plan, then?"

"If you'll give us the keys, Peter and I will investigate at the flat and see if we can find any evidence. We may even surprise the smugglers at their work." He drew the mystery key from his pocket and handed it to Reynolds. "This key arrived tonight, and I think it may be to the flat. We may be walking into a trap."

"That sounds dangerous."

"I was in the army. I'm not concerned."

Reynolds slapped his hands on the surface of the desk and rose to his feet. "It's my property, and I don't want it damaged. I'll come with you."

Philip nodded, relieved to have additional assistance along with Reynolds' knowledge of the territory ahead. "We need to leave as soon as possible. I think they let you go because they're nearly done with whatever it is they're doing."

Reynolds left the room to fetch his overcoat while Philip paced, eager for action now that he had made up his mind. Peter watched him from his seat, an unusually thoughtful expression on his face.

"You know Mother will have a fit if you marry that man's daughter."

"I don't care," Philip said. "We've never agreed on anything. Besides, Mother has terrible matchmaking taste. Did you ever meet that schoolroom miss she was trying to get Paul to marry before the chit ran away? It would have been a worse mismatch than Prinny and Princess Caroline."

"She won't be the only one who shuns you."

Philip turned to face his brother full on. In his martial mood, he felt well up for the confrontation. Better to discuss it now and know where he stood.

"Will you be one of the ones who shun us?"

"No," Peter said after a long moment of introspection. "I may not approve, but I could never abandon you."

Philip took three strides forward and clapped his brother on the shoulder. "That's all the support I'll need, then."

Junia peeked through the curtains of her bedroom as the men exited the house, once again using the kitchen door. Poor Mrs. Higgins would be angry to have her routine interrupted twice in one night. Even Mama was reluctant to risk their cook and housekeeper's wrath when Mrs. Higgins felt her domain was being interfered with.

Dusk was gathering quickly, and the three men were soon out of sight. Her eavesdropping had been incomplete, but it seemed they planned to search the flat and then hide in place to see if they could confirm who the smugglers were.

She knew she ought to stay safely home and wait for the

men to return. It was what Philip would want, and what her parents would expect.

But the same cold knot that had formed in her stomach when she witnessed her father's abduction was forming again. She needed to listen to that instinct more than she needed to be obedient.

"What are you doing?"

Junia started and spun around as Zillah came into the room. "Shh! Close the door."

Puzzled but willing, Zillah obeyed before crossing to the window and peering over Junia's shoulder. "Are they leaving?"

"Yes," Junia said, "and I don't like it."

She went to their wardrobe and pulled out a dark cloak.

"You're not going to follow them, are you?"

"I don't need to follow them," Junia said, with a bravado she did not entirely feel. "I know where they're going. I just need to… arrive a little later than they do."

"I'm going with you."

"You can't. You need to stay with Mama."

"Mama will be fine with Mrs. Higgins and Sally in the house. I'm coming with you. You know it's dangerous for a woman to be alone on the streets at night."

"It's dangerous for two women, too."

"But not *as* dangerous." Zillah pulled her own cloak from the wardrobe. "Come on. Let's go save Pappa."

PHILIP SCANNED the street both as they walked up to the building and as Reynolds unlocked the side door that led to the staircase up to the flat. He did not see anything, but the itch at the back of his neck told him not to be complacent. Danger hovered just out of sight. He could feel it.

"Would someone else be able to get the extra key to the flat?" Philip kept his voice low so as not to carry past the three of them.

"Easily, if they were dishonest," Reynolds said, his voice equally quiet. "It's kept hanging next to the chief clerk's desk."

Inside the darkened flat, there was just enough light for Philip to see shrouded shapes which could be mistaken for furniture with holland covers on top. He lifted the edge of one sheet to see that what lay underneath was not a settee, as the shape might indicate, but a series of crates stacked into the right shape.

Reynolds whistled softly as he surveyed the room. "We took every stick of furniture with us when we moved to the house."

"That was what Junia said." Philip walked to each grouping of boxes, peering under the cover of each to confirm they were all crates, not furniture.

"What do they have in there?" Reynolds asked.

"Likely tea," Peter said. "It's one of the most profitable things to smuggle. Could be some fabrics and laces as well." He spoke with the authority of a man who had been ministering to sailors for months and had heard all of their secret confessions.

Philip did another circuit of the room, walking slowly. "From what I understand, smugglers do most of their business in the markets at the edge of town rather than risking bringing their goods directly into the city. So what are they doing here?"

"Looks like you're about to find out, parson."

Philip froze at the familiar, sneering voice behind him and turned slowly, cursing his rusty skills. He should have remembered to check the kitchen to prevent Dickie from ambushing them.

Dickie stood with a branch of lit candles in one hand and a flintlock pistol in the other. The big man who had a soft spot for Junia—Robby, his name was—stood at Dickie's shoulder pointing his own pistol at Philip.

Reynolds turned as well, glancing at Philip as he raised his hands. Philip prevented himself from looking around. He was fairly certain he had heard a soft thud as Peter dropped to the ground, so he wanted to keep the two villains focused on himself and Reynolds.

"You've been a lot of trouble to us, parson," Dickie said, "but that ends tonight."

"Do you intend to kill us?"

"No need for us to do it. We'll leave you here after we take the goods and let Smythe's men deal with you. They'll be in a temper for sure, missing us and losing their goods all together."

A clatter of more footsteps on the stairs made Dickie glance away, but not long enough for Philip to make a move. It was no surprise when Hughes and Williams appeared in the doorway, herded by Jasper and Jem. Hughes in particular looked far less self-assured than he had in the Reynolds drawing room, and he immediately turned a pleading look on Dickie, who set the candleholder down on one of the stacks of covered crates.

"Please, uncle," Hughes said. "I don't understand why you need us here. We gave you everything!"

Dickie rolled his eyes and spat at Hughes' feet. "'Uncle,' ye call me now that you're in trouble. You and yer pap wouldn't give me the time of day 'til yer needed me."

Hughes subsided, and Williams kept his head down, clearly miserable. The other two men started a slow trek around the room, poking suspiciously at the covered crates.

Out of the corner of his eye, Philip saw movement. Peter rose, half-crouched, from his hiding spot and began edging his way behind the group, but he stumbled on an uneven floorboard and Jasper whirled to confront him. He stared in disbelief, looking between Philip and Peter until understanding dawned in his eyes.

"Bloody hell," Jasper said. "They're twins!"

Dickie cuffed him on the side of the head without looking away from Philip, who he clearly judged to be the more dangerous of the two brothers. "Of course they're twins! And you went and nabbed the wrong one."

"You was there too, Dickie," Jasper said with surprising dignity. "I didn't hear you saying not to do it."

"It's no matter now," Dickie said. "But we can't be the ones to kill them. The excise would never stop looking for us if we killed one dook's son, much less two of 'em."

Jasper and Dickie looked to where Hughes and Williams hovered at the edge of the room. The two younger men were clearly debating whether or not they ought to try and make a run for it despite Robby's bulk between them and the stairs.

Philip thought he heard the soft scrape of a foot near the half-open door to the stairs and coughed loudly to try and drown it out. Robby glared at him, but looked uncertainly in the direction of the noise, clearly torn between guarding them and going to look for the source.

JUNIA RAN down the stairs as quickly and quietly as she could and met a nervous Zillah outside. "They've taken Philip and Pappa prisoner. We need to go fetch Mr. Force. He'll know what to do."

The Force home was nearly a mile away, but Junia and Zillah lifted their skirts to their knees and ran, ignoring the passers-by who stared at them. They ran up the front stairs where Junia pounded on the front door until a footman opened it.

"What are you making that noise for? Go away!"

Junia stuck her boot-clad foot in the door. "We must speak to Mr. Force immediately. Caius Reynolds—my father —is in danger and needs his help."

The footman hesitated at the familiar name, and then reluctantly opened the door to let them into the foyer to wait. Junia stood as patiently as she could while Zillah looked around the grand house with wide eyes.

"Miss Reynolds?" a voice said, and Junia turned in relief to see Thaddeus Force descending the stairs. He was in his early thirties, a handsome man of mixed race, his voice still carrying a trace of his birthplace in Italy. Within only a few years of his arrival in England, and with the help of aristocratic connections that included the new Duchess of Livesay, he was one of the most successful importers of fabrics and laces in London.

Junia curtsied to him, and elbowed Zillah to do the same. "May we speak in private, Mr. Force? It's an urgent matter."

"Of course." He ushered them up the stairs and into his study, where he settled them into the chairs in front of his desk.

"If you will, Miss Reynolds."

Junia took a deep breath. "It all started when my father was abducted…"

Mr. Force listened intently as Junia related her story as quickly as possible, raising his eyebrows when she mentioned Philip and Peter Avondale.

"Sometimes," he said, "I forget how small London can be."

"Philip—Major Avondale—thought the culprit could be one of my father's clerks, and he was right."

Mr. Force rose to his feet. "There's no time to lose. We must go at once."

"WE'RE NOT MURDERERS, JACK," Williams hissed.

"We're not, but *they* are," Hughes muttered back, gesturing to the men gathered around the shrouded crates. "It'll be them or us that gets killed, and I don't want it to be us."

"Why did I listen to you in the first place?"

"Because you got greedy, just like me," Hughes said. "We're not going to make as much as we hoped, but if we can take care of this… little problem, we'll still walk away with a profit."

Philip was fairly certain the two younger men didn't

realize he could hear them. This had never been a clever scheme, but idiotic schemes were just as likely to get one killed as clever ones. Maybe even more so.

The rope they had been tied with scraped his wrists as he pulled and stretched his bonds as discreetly as he could. Glancing over at Reynolds, he could see the older man doing the same with grim determination. He was concerned about Peter, but even the most hardened smuggler should be reluctant to harm a clergyman. At least, Philip hoped so.

Just as one wrist slipped free of his bonds, he saw Williams and Hughes finish their dispute and look over to where he and Reynolds sat. He glared back at them, discreetly shifting so he blocked Reynolds from their view as the man continued to struggle with the rope that bound his hands.

Hughes took a deep breath and stepped forward with the pistol Dickie had pressed into his shaking hand. Even as he began to raise it, Philip sprang at him and seized his wrist, twisting hard until the smaller man cried out and dropped the gun. Williams took a swing at him and Philip ducked, pulling Hughes' arm behind him as Philip used the other man as a shield.

"That's enough!" Dickie barked, and Philip turned to see the smuggler with his arm around Peter's neck, half-bending his brother to the ground with a gun at Peter's temple. "Leggo or I blow the parson's brains out."

Slowly, Philip loosened his grip and Hughes staggered away. Dickie raised his gun to point at Philip even as Robby, standing at the window, frowned at what he saw outside.

"There's men outside," Robby said.

"What do you mean, there's men outside? Which men?"

Robby shrugged. "Dunno. Just men."

Dickie shoved Peter away and gestured to Philip. "C'mere." When he hesitated, Dickie gestured more urgently. "Come 'ere, or I'll shoot ye where you stand."

Reluctantly, Philip came within arm's reach, and Dickie pushed him toward the stairs. "You go first. I'm right behind you with the gun. If they shoot, they'll get you first."

Dickie formed the rest into a rough line, with Reynolds, Peter, Williams, and Hughes in the middle guarded by Jasper and Jem, and Robby bringing up the rear. "If it's the Kentish gang come to claim their goods, they'll shoot you first and we'll have time to run. If it's the excise men, we can say we'll shoot the hostages and they'll have to let us go. Move it, now."

His hands raised, Philip led the way down the stairs, Dickie's pistol cold at his ear as the other man reached past him to open the door.

As the door opened, Philip was momentarily blinded by lights outside, but he knew Dickie must be, too. Dropping to his knees, he rolled through the doorway while kicking out, catching Dickie by surprise. He landed a solid blow, and the gun went flying as Dickie lost his balance from the well-placed kick to his knee and fell, cursing all the way down. As he fell, Peter and Reynolds dove through the door and off to each side, leaving Jasper and Jem exposed to whatever awaited them outside. A tense silence followed, punctuated only by Dickie's howls of pain as he clutched his injured knee. As Philip watched, the rest of the gang slowly dropped their weapons and raised their hands in surrender.

Philip rolled to his feet, and crouched to face what the gang had seen, ready to continue the fight. To his relief, he immediately recognized Thaddeus Force, who led a group of torch-carrying excise men and local merchants that blocked any escape route for the would-be smugglers. As Philip straightened, Junia rushed forward from the back of the crowd, and he caught her in his arms as she leapt towards him, her face glowing.

"You're all right! And Pappa!"

"And my brother, too," Philip said. Conscious of the men surrounding them, he kissed her forehead and put her a little away from him, though he kept his left arm around her waist.

Force stepped forward and nodded. "Major Avondale."

Philip grinned at him. "Glad to see you again, Force. Relieved, I have to admit. Thank you for your help."

Force bowed, but Philip extended his right hand instead. After a moment's hesitation, the other man shook it firmly, as an equal.

Aware of the observing crowd, Philip looked around and saw Zillah had made her way to her father's side and was fussing over him as he soothed her. Philip knew standing on a public street like this with his arm around Junia, surrounded by her community, was a declaration of intent on his part. Now he only needed to convince Junia. And her mama.

He raised his voice a little and said, "Thank you, gentlemen. Your assistance was very timely."

Philip turned to see Robby had herded the rest of the smugglers to the excise men and was shaking hands all around. Robby looked over at Philip and nodded, his eyes grazing wistfully over Junia before he turned back to the rest of the excise men. It seemed Junia had not been the only one in the house working against the kidnappers.

Junia seemed to suddenly realize they had an audience

and stepped away so hastily that he needed to steady her with a hand on her elbow. He took her hand and tucked it into the crook of his arm as they led the procession back to the Reynolds house to relieve her mother's mind, while the smugglers were led away by the excise men, including Robby. Philip wondered if he would ever find out what the tale was there.

The group was in a celebratory mood as they returned to the house, with Mrs. Higgins and an excited Sally passing glasses of punch and mugs of ale to the group for a toast or two in the entryway before Philip and Caius Reynolds began to edge everyone towards the door. Thaddeus Force was clearly as eager to return to his own snug home as Mrs. Reynolds was to return order to her household and did his part to help disperse the exhilarated crowd of merchants.

He and Philip shook hands one more time, and Force and Peter exchanged bows.

"Thank you, Mr. Force," Mrs. Reynolds said, and he bowed to her as well.

"I am happy to be of assistance, ma'am. Good night."

Mrs. Reynolds gathered her two daughters and led them upstairs, Junia glancing back at Philip only once before she followed in her mother's wake. He watched her go with a pang, uncertain even now if his addresses would be welcome when he made them.

Peter shifted from foot to foot, and Philip clapped him on the shoulder. "Why don't you head back to the flat? I'll meet you there in a bit."

Peter looked from Philip to Reynolds and back again, and then sighed deeply. "You've made up your mind?"

"After tonight, you still have to ask that? Yes, I've made up my mind."

Peter bowed his good night to both of them, and Reynolds closed the front door behind him. The entryway was suddenly silent, with the excitement of the evening's events left behind.

"Let's go up to my office, Major Avondale. I've got whiskey there."

"I could use some," Philip said ruefully, and let Junia's father lead the way.

Once upstairs, Philip accepted his glass and took a seat on the visitor side of the desk. Caius Reynolds set his untouched glass down on the surface of the desk and took his seat. He regarded Philip without expression for a long moment.

"She's a good girl, our Junia," her father said at last, "sweet and dutiful. But once she makes up her mind, she's as stubborn as an old mule."

"I know," Philip said, and the two men exchanged an exasperated smile.

"Well, in this case, she's made her mind up to have you, and nothing on heaven or earth will be able to change her mind, no matter how her mother and I feel about it."

"I can't say I haven't had any hesitations," Philip admitted. "Some people I know will likely shun us, or be cruel to us, and there may be some you know who will do the same. But I have every intention of sheltering and cherishing your daughter for the rest of our lives, and as long as the people closest to us accept our marriage, I think we can defy the rest of the world. Together."

Reynolds looked at Philip for a long moment and then, at last, he smiled. "You know," he said, "I think you two just might be able to do that."

Junia accepted her mother's drawing room scolding with good grace and only half her attention, the other half still standing in the street with Philip's protective arm around her, knowing he was safe, and Pappa was safe, and the smugglers had been arrested.

And knowing he had stayed behind to speak to Pappa.

"Are you listening to anything I say, Junia?" her mother asked in exasperation.

Junia started. "I… um…"

They all looked up as the door opened to see Pappa standing there. He smiled at Junia.

"He's waiting for you in my study."

Mama looked from one to the other of them and sighed in resignation even as Zillah began to giggle with glee, stifling the sound with her hand.

Pappa extended his hand to help his wife up from the settee and plant a kiss on her cheek. "Don't worry so much, honey. They'll be fine."

"I hope so," Mama said in a dire tone, but allowed him to lead her towards their room, Zillah trailing behind.

As Junia started walking to the study, her mother's words from the foot of the stairs halted her. "I know the horses have already gone, but leave the door open. I want to at least *pretend* you all did this properly."

With an irresistible surge of elation, Junia rushed to her parents and embraced them, kissing each of them on the cheek in turn. "It will be fine, Mama. We'll be fine."

Mama pulled her close for a moment and then gave her a little push back towards the study. "Don't leave that man waiting."

Junia made sure to keep her steps as measured and dignified as she could manage when she wanted to run into the room and jump into Philip's arms. She opened the study door and he turned from the fireplace to smile at her, extending his hands to her.

Then she did run, and he caught her against him, crushing her in his arms until she giggled a protest.

"If you ever—and I mean *ever*—put yourself in danger like that again," he vowed, "I will spank you like the hoyden you are."

"Yes, Philip." She pulled back a little and looked up at him, knowing she was starry-eyed, and he smiled down at her, his fierce expression softening.

"I spoke to your father," he said, and her heart expanded even more.

"I know."

"It won't be easy."

"I know that, too."

He let go of her, only to frame her face in his hands.

"I love you, Junia Reynolds. Marry me?"

"Yes," she said, or tried to, because he kissed her almost before she could get the word out, passion flaring between them immediately as she wound her arms around his neck and he pulled her hips against his.

Until, that is, someone cleared their throat from the open doorway, and they turned to see a wide-eyed Zillah standing there.

"Mama sent me back down to make sure you behave yourselves before the wedding," Zillah said. "So *behave yourselves*."

EPILOGUE
THE FOLLOWING SUMMER

A high-pitched screech was Philip's only warning before his brother-in-law, George, flung himself headlong into Philip's arms. With a roar, he lifted George into the air and tossed him skyward as the child giggled uncontrollably. Tucking the wiggling boy under his arm, Philip looked for Junia, who was walking towards them with her youngest sister Sophia, who had progressed to toddling around while safely holding another's hands.

"Mama asked me to bring them outside," Junia explained. "And as soon as Sophie saw the garden, she wanted to walk."

As if on cue, George began protesting and struggling to get down. Philip set him on his feet so he could join his sisters. Sophia pulled her hands away from Junia's and toddled a few steps on her own before falling onto her cushioned bottom in front of a clump of daisies. George joined her on the grass, accepting the flowers she plucked and handed to him with a comically grave air.

Junia moved close, and Philip slipped his arm around her

waist, letting his hand rest on the gentle swell of her stomach. It had not been an easy year for either of them. He had been rejected by some of his old friends and comrades, who could not understand why he would marry a woman so far beneath him. As he had expected, his mother had refused her blessing and ignored their marriage, though his siblings had rallied around. Some of Junia's London friends had turned their backs as well, though they kept their opinions quiet when Mr. Force and his wife Maria showed their support.

Once Philip and Junia had settled into their country house after their marriage, the visits began. The servants had been thrown into a tizzy by the arrival of the Duke and Duchess of Livesey, Philip's oldest brother Paul and his wife Olivia. Peter and his new wife Georgiana had stopped to visit during their wedding tour and the brothers had reconnected while Junia and Georgie became fast friends who now corresponded regularly.

His in-laws had arrived yesterday for a long visit to escape the smoke and crowds of London and filled the house with warmth and laughter. If Caius and Jerusha Reynolds still held any reservations about the marriage, those seemed to be gone now. Zillah had made her debut in their small society of merchants earlier that spring and declared she needed an escape from her many suitors, none of whom seemed to interest her in the least so far.

"Shall we tell them tonight?" Philip said, giving Junia's belly another gentle caress, and she turned to smile up at him.

"Yes. Let's tell them tonight." She lay her hand on his, on top of where their child was growing, and they watched George and Sophia play in their garden.

It's not often I get an idea directly from something I find while doing research, but in this case, Peter Snow's 2014 nonfiction book about the War of 1812, *When Britain Burned the White House*, gave me the seed of this story.

The book contained several passages describing how, when British troops traveled up the Chesapeake Bay to attack Washington D.C. and Baltimore, hundreds of enslaved people took refuge with them and were brought back to England on British troopships to begin their new lives as free people. As in the American Revolution, the American government tried to demand the return of this "property" during the negotiations to settle the War of 1812 but, as in the earlier war, Britain steadfastly refused to return people to slavery and all who wished to do so remained in Great Britain.

According to records kept by the British Navy, it was not only individuals who escaped, but families as well. Most indications are these newly free people settled into the existing Black British communities in London, Bristol, and other port cities. In the Regency Era, it is estimated there were between 5,000 to 10,000 people of African descent living in London alone, with more scattered around the country. For the most part, people in the Georgian and Regency Eras lived according to social class rather than along racial lines, so there were small enclaves within similar social classes rather than large neighborhoods segregated by race as in the United States.

Interracial marriage outside the upper classes was not uncommon and was never banned for anyone in Great Britain. It was less common in the upper class, but not unheard of—in the Georgian Era, a younger son of the Earl of Fyfe married one of the mixed-race Jamaican heiresses I alluded to, as documented in Daniel Livesay's 2018 book *Children of Uncertain Fortune*.

Because written records are sketchy, I have imagined a small community of formerly enslaved Londoners acting much like other immigrant communities have throughout history, banding together to help each other in times of trouble and stand against outside forces, and further imagined one of them might be able to have a Cinderella story in her new country with the handsome British officer who helped transport her family to safety in England.

ACKNOWLEDGMENTS

I want to thank my developmental editor at A Book A Day, Regina Lofton McKinney, who read the manuscript twice to make sure I didn't mess up the Black characters I wanted to include. I also want to thank my beta readers, Lisa Cody, Shanti Mercer, and Caro Kincaid, the latter of whom allowed me to pay her in the yarn I was destashing from our apartment. Whitney Jones Francis at Empowered Writing took on the task of helping me expand and polish the story as a stand-alone novella after its first publication in 2023's limited-time anthology *The Regency Abduction Club*.

This was a pretty scary book to write, and I thank every person who encouraged me to go for it and didn't immediately think me writing a heroine who had grown up enslaved was an absolutely terrible idea.

And, as always, I thank my husband, who tells me both when my ideas are terrible and when they're great.

ABOUT THE AUTHOR

Alexa Santi loves storytelling of all kinds, so it's no wonder it took some time for her to settle on romance fiction after several detours that included an MFA in Screenwriting. She lives near Los Angeles with her sexy archivist husband and their pesky cats, who insist she take frequent breaks from her writing to pay attention to them. You can find her on Facebook, Instagram, Linktree, or on her website at https://www.alexasanti.com/

Want to hear what I'm doing next? Sign up for my newsletter either on my website or at https://www.subscribepage.com/alexasanti